"What were you doing with, Riley?"

The little girl giggled. "I told him that I don't think you know anything about starting a camp. But he probably does since he's out in the woods a lot."

"Funny girl." Janie grabbed the bag of food resting on the back seat. "I hope everyone is hungry. We've got enough food here to feed the entire town."

"Let's hurry up and go inside," Riley called out as she reached for Drew's hand. "I can't wait for you to meet our dog."

Janie observed her daughter and Drew with reservations.

The last thing she wanted was for her daughter to get attached to him. But what about her? Growing up, they'd been the best of friends, but they'd never dated. She'd had a secret crush on him. That was all. Still, she needed to keep her feelings in check. Drew was simply honoring Mrs. Applegate's wishes to help with the camp, so he could take control of his portion of the land.

Nothing more.

When it came to Drew Brenner, Janie would need to keep her guard up...

Weekdays, **Jill Weatherholt** works for the City of Charlotte. On the weekend, she writes contemporary stories about love, faith and forgiveness. Raised in the suburbs of Washington, DC, she now resides in North Carolina. She holds a degree in psychology from George Mason University and a paralegal studies certification from Duke University. She shares her life with her real-life hero and number one supporter. Jill loves connecting with readers at jillweatherholt.com.

Books by Jill Weatherholt

Love Inspired

Second Chance Romance
A Father for Bella
A Mother for His Twins
A Home for Her Daughter

Visit the Author Profile page at Harlequin.com.

A Home
for Her Daughter

Jill Weatherholt

LOVE INSPIRED

INSPIRATIONAL ROMANCE

LOVE INSPIRED®
INSPIRATIONAL ROMANCE

Recycling programs for this product may not exist in your area.

ISBN-13: 978-1-335-48838-1

A Home for Her Daughter

This edition published by arrangement with Harlequin Books S.A.

For questions and comments about the quality of this book, please contact us at CustomerService@Harlequin.com.

Love Inspired
22 Adelaide St. West, 40th Floor
Toronto, Ontario M5H 4E3, Canada
www.Harlequin.com

Printed in U.S.A.

A man's heart deviseth his way:
but the Lord directeth his steps.
—*Proverbs* 16:9

To my beautiful niece, Janie, your enthusiasm
for my books and encouragement help to push
me through those times of self-doubt. I love you.

Acknowledgments

Until I published my first book,
I was clueless as to the number of hardworking
people it takes to bring a story to life. Two of
those people are my agent, Jessica Alvarez of
BookEnds Literary Agency, and my editor,
Dina Davis. Thank you both for believing in
my stories and guiding me on this journey.

Chapter One

Early Tuesday morning, Drew Brenner sat in the reception area of the Caldwell and Richardson law firm, one of two firms in Whispering Slopes—not exactly where he wanted to be on his day off. He hadn't stepped foot inside this office since the day after he buried his family. It hadn't changed a bit. A light coating of dust covered the artificial ficus tree in the corner. A stack of outdated magazines fanned the top of the cherry coffee table.

A shudder rippled through him. Thankfully, Mrs. Wingo's mahogany desk, with a blank sign-in sheet on top, sat empty this morning. He wasn't in the mood for small talk. The ticking pendulum clock on the wall struck nine o'clock and within seconds the door behind the receptionist's desk opened.

"Drew, it's good to see you." Larry Caldwell, a portly, elderly man strolled across the hardwood floor with his hand extended. "It's been a while. How are you doing, son?"

Larry had been a close family friend. As a little boy, Drew's parents often invited him and his wife over for

Sunday dinner. He'd always worn a suit and today was no different. Did he ever dress in casual clothing?

"I can't complain." Drew removed his hat and shook the wrinkled yet strong hand. He found comfort in the man's presence.

The lawyer gave Drew a once-over. "Since it's obvious by the uniform that you're working today, we'll take care of this as quickly as possible. Go ahead and take a seat in the conference room. The other party should be here shortly. I'll go see if I can figure out the coffee maker. Mrs. Wingo is coming in late today, so I'm all out of sorts." He scurried off toward the small kitchenette, and wooden cabinets opening and slamming closed echoed down the hall.

Typically, Drew didn't wear his ranger uniform outside of the park, but he had a tight schedule this morning. There'd be no time to go home and change before his shift. He headed toward the conference room, pulling a peppermint from his pocket. After removing the wrapper, he popped the mint into his mouth. The cooling sensation always settled his nerves.

Who else in Whispering Slopes had been named in Mary Applegate's will? When the sweet lady had passed away last month, she'd left instructions that there would be no funeral or service. Drew only learned about her death when he'd received a certified letter in the mail informing him he'd been designated a beneficiary in her will.

The bell over the front door chimed, and voices carried down the hall and into the conference room. Larry spoke, but Drew couldn't make out what was being said as the discussion grew closer.

When the new arrival entered the room, Drew looked up from the certified letter resting in front of him and did a double take. His breath caught in his throat. *Janie Capello*. He hadn't seen her since her family moved to Chicago their sophomore year in high school, but he'd never forgotten her. Those sparkling green eyes and rich caramel hair were a dead giveaway. His mouth felt like asphalt under a blazing late-August sun as her eyes met his. Of course Mrs. Applegate would name Janie in her will. It made perfect sense. She'd been like a mother to Janie.

"Drew, you remember Janie Capello—sorry, it's Edmiston now—don't you?"

Stunned, Drew nodded.

"I'll go check on the coffee while you two get reacquainted." Larry shuffled out the door.

Janie's fingers touched her parted lips. "Drew? I didn't expect to see you here." She glided across the room, glancing toward the hardwood floor.

Drew stood to greet his old friend. She briefly stepped into his embrace, but when her body tensed, he retreated. "It's good to see you, Janie." He smiled.

"Let me take your jacket," he offered.

"No! I'm fine."

Drew didn't respond to Janie's curt reply. "So who is this?" He glanced down at the child holding Janie's hand and his heart squeezed. Her blond hair and pixie cut sparked a memory of his own little girl.

"I'm Riley Edmiston." She grinned, revealing a missing front tooth. "I just turned seven. Do you have any kids my age?" She looked up, her almond-colored eyes full of hopefulness.

Gazing downward, he could only shake his head.

"Oh rats. I was hoping to meet some new people. I

had lots of friends when we lived in Maryland. I didn't want to move, but Mommy said we had to."

Drew turned to Janie as though looking for confirmation.

"That's right. My brother finally convinced us to move. You're looking at the two newest residents of Whispering Slopes." Janie glanced at Riley. "Until I find a place for us, we'll be staying at Nick's house."

Drew had always liked her brother Nick. He had been a senior in high school when her family moved, but he'd returned to Whispering Slopes to start a new life after losing his first wife. "I don't see much of Nick and his family. How are they doing?"

"Actually, they all left two days ago for a mission trip to Ethiopia. They'll be gone for three months." Janie flashed a satisfied grin. "With this being such a small town, I'm surprised you don't run into Nick often."

Since the accident two years ago, Drew kept to himself. "My house is off Hawkeye Trail. That's where I work, too, so I don't come into town much." If he avoided all types of relationships, he wouldn't suffer any more heartache. At least that's what he kept telling himself.

Janie's beautiful eyes connected with his. "So you work in law enforcement?"

A job that required being alone most of the time, which was exactly what he wanted. "I'm a park ranger. I got my park administration degree online a couple of years ago." After the accident, he'd given up his job as a paramedic. How could he expect to help strangers when he couldn't even save his own family?

Riley moved in closer to Drew and crinkled her nose. "So you're like the Smokey Bear guy?"

Drew laughed. "Yeah, something like that."

The little girl continued to stare. "You seem nice. Maybe you can be my friend. I only have one so far. Her name is Leslie." She exhaled as she looked up at Drew.

Larry stepped inside the room carrying a tray with three coffee cups. He placed it in the middle of the table. "Hopefully it isn't too strong. There's plenty of cream and sugar if it is." He turned his attention to Riley. "I put out a couple of coloring books and crayons on Mrs. Wingo's desk, Riley. Is that okay, Janie?"

"Of course." Janie rested her hand on her daughter's shoulder. "Riley, go color while the grown-ups meet."

"Okay, Mommy." The child skipped through the doorway and down the hall.

The attorney looked to Janie. "I locked the front door, so don't worry."

"Thank you." Janie reached for her beverage, poured a splash of cream and took a sip before settling back in the leather chair. "Mmm...it's perfect."

"It looks like we can begin going over Mary Applegate's estate." Carrying a thick file, Larry took a seat at the head of the table and placed the documents in front of him.

Janie glanced sideways at Drew. "I still can't believe she's gone. She was such a loving and caring woman."

Larry reached over and patted Janie's hand. "I'm afraid we all lost a special friend last month. Fortunately, Mary passed peacefully in her sleep."

Drew watched while Janie brushed her palm down her cheek. "You okay?"

Janie shook her head. "I should have made more of an effort to keep in touch. For years, I called her once a week to check in with her. But then—"

"Don't be so hard on yourself. We all have busy lives…plus you were living hundreds of miles away. She knew how much you cared about her." Larry shuffled the stack of papers in front of him. "That will become clear to you once we go over her estate."

Why hadn't they stayed in touch? Before Janie moved away, she and Mrs. Applegate had been like mother and daughter. Then again, he'd been close to Janie too, but never stayed in contact.

Larry took a sip of his coffee. "I've made copies for each of you since you're both named as beneficiaries." He passed a document to Janie and then another to Drew. "As you both know, Mrs. Applegate had no living relatives. Over the years, she and I had a lot of conversations. I know for a fact she thought of you both as her family."

Janie whimpered. "After my mother became lost in addiction, Mrs. Applegate stepped in and filled her shoes. She did so much for me. And then we had to move."

"She loved you like a daughter, Janie. And that's the reason she's left most of her estate to you. She wanted to be assured that you and Riley are well taken care of," Larry explained as he looked over the rim of his thick-framed glasses.

Drew pushed away from the table, walked over to the credenza and picked up a box of tissues. Heading back to his seat, he offered the box to Janie.

She plucked a tissue from the flowered container and dabbed each eye. "Thank you. This is really hard for me." She softly blew her nose. "If it wasn't for Mrs. Applegate, I don't think I would have survived the past ten years."

Drew's attention focused on her words. What kind of life had she lived in Maryland?

The attorney cleared his throat and resumed reading the document. "You can see on page three how she's divided her specific gifts to each of you. Her savings and all other monetary accounts are listed."

Drew took note of the large sum of money that had been set aside for Riley's college tuition. That should give Janie some peace of mind. Knowing what a financial burden college could be to a family, this made him happy.

"Drew, she's specified some personal items she'd like for you to have along with seventy-five acres." For a second, he thought about what he might have done with the land if his life hadn't changed so drastically. Would he have finally opened that outdoor adventure facility? Once upon a time, it had been a goal for him.

Larry eyed Drew. "Are you okay, son? You look a little pale."

"I'm fine." Images flooded his mind. He and Janie, along with the other children, roasting marshmallows over the open fire as Mr. Applegate played his guitar. Those summers spent at Rocky River Camp had been some of the happiest in his life.

The antique cherry grandfather clock sitting in the corner of the room struck half past the hour.

"The remaining land, over two hundred acres, along with the farmhouse, will go to you, Janie." He turned to her and gave her a single nod.

She gasped. "The house?" Janie wiped away the tears pooling her eyes. "Riley and I will have a home?"

Drew wasn't sure if Janie realized the monetary extent of her inheritance. Over the years, Mrs. Applegate had mentioned to him that numerous developers had approached her about selling the land nestled within the Shenandoah Valley. It was prime real estate.

Slowly, Larry removed his glasses and placed them on the table. He carefully closed the file and clasped his hands in front of him. "There are some conditions Mary has specified in order to take ownership of your respective portions of the property."

Janie turned to Drew and raised her brow before turning away. "Why would Mrs. Applegate do that?"

"It goes along with some of her last wishes." Larry's voice cracked.

The papers crinkled as Drew fingered through the will feeling as though he held Mrs. Applegate's life in his hands. She and her husband had built a beautiful life together in Virginia's Shenandoah Valley. A sense of peace filled Drew's heart knowing the two were together once again.

"I'd like to hear those wishes, Larry." Janie spoke in a whisper.

He nodded and looked down at the table: "First of all, Janie, she wants you to reopen the Rocky River Camp you loved so much as a child. She's made provisions to pay for the cost of labor and materials. Also, the insurance premium will be paid until you take ownership. She didn't want to put any unnecessary financial burden on you." The lawyer paused and glanced at both beneficiaries before turning his attention back to the will. "And Drew, in order for you to take possession of the seventy-five acres, you must sign this document promising to help Janie get the camp up and running for the Fourth of July."

Drew tightened his jaw. "That's only a few weeks away."

"I know it doesn't give you two much time, but the Fourth was a special day for Mrs. Applegate."

No matter how distinct the day was to her, Drew

had a job. He didn't have time for this. "What made it so special?"

"That's the day she and her husband were married. It would have been sixty years. Also, it will be the fortieth anniversary of the camp's grand opening." Larry rubbed his brow. "I'm sorry, but those are her terms."

For a second, Drew wasn't sure if he was still breathing. What was he being pulled into? He couldn't give up his safety and solitude for seventy-five acres. Helping Janie would only bring him more heartache. How could he be around Riley—a child who would be the exact age of his own, had he been able to save her?

"Are you going to sign the document?" Janie's clammy hand dropped the pen on the table. She watched as it rolled off onto the floor. Clenching her fists, she struggled to keep her emotions in check.

Larry cleared his throat and focused his attention on Drew. "What's the problem, son? Mrs. Applegate wanted to leave her land to someone who would love it as much as she did."

Janie's mind raced. She and Riley would have a home of their own. One filled with love—a peaceful refuge from her past life. She'd been too embarrassed to tell her brother she had little money in savings, thanks to her ex-husband and his high-powered attorney.

But how could she handle the inheritance if Drew didn't agree to the terms? After the divorce and up until the move, Janie worked as a writer and travel photographer with a local magazine. It was what she'd always dreamed of doing, but the money wasn't great and it became more difficult for her to leave Riley.

Maybe her ex-husband was right about her lack of

abilities. She couldn't get the camp up and running on her own, not without Drew's help. Even Mrs. Applegate obviously believed that. She'd loved the camp as a child, but the behind-the-scenes operation of it all? She was clueless as to what Mrs. Applegate and her husband had done to ensure every child who visited left with sweet memories.

Drew stroked his hand over the top of his head, squirming in his seat. "It's just—I already have a job. I don't know how I would have the time." He squared his broad shoulders when Janie cast a pleading look in his direction.

She swiped her finger over the documents in front of her. On these pages were her dear friend's last wishes and, with or without Drew's help, she'd make Rocky River Camp the best on the East Coast. *Okay. Just breathe.* A sense of calm took hold and she turned to the attorney. "I can do this on my own. I don't need his help." Janie tilted her head in Drew's direction.

"Well, I'm afraid you do. The will specifically states that if Drew doesn't agree to the terms and they're not met by the Fourth, then all of the land will be put up for auction and the proceeds will go to the Alzheimer's Association."

Janie's chin trembled at Larry's words.

"What about the money for Riley's college tuition?" His voice shook. "And the house?" Drew turned from Janie to the lawyer and then back to her.

"All of it goes to charity." Larry looked down at the papers.

With those words, Janie's stomach lurched before Drew picked up the black ink pen and began to sign the pages.

An hour later, with all of the documents signed, the two old friends and Riley crossed the parking lot of the law firm. Drew placed his hat on his head.

"So do people think you look like the guy from Smokey Bear, Mr. Drew?" Her daughter grinned.

Drew laughed. "I guess some do. I'm heading to work at the park this morning."

"That's cool you get to work at a park! Maybe we can come visit you." Riley squealed and waved her arms while jumping up and down. "Can we, Mommy?"

"We'll see," Janie responded, looking up. The early June sun was filtered through a thin veil of clouds. A buttermilk sky. That's what her mother used to call it.

Heaviness gripped Janie's limbs at the thought that Drew had agreed to the terms against his will—but why? She stopped with a jerk and reached for his arm. "Why did you change your mind?" Her chin quivered. "What about your job?"

"Mommy, if you and Mr. Drew are going to talk grown-up stuff, can you unlock the car so I can read? Fern is trying to think of a way to save Wilbur. It's so exciting!" Riley beamed.

Drew laughed. "That was one of my favorite books when I was a kid. I begged my father to buy me a pig."

Riley giggled, dancing a little jig. "Really? I've always wanted a pig, too."

Janie fished into her purse for the car keys and popped the lock. "Go ahead, sweetie. I'll be a few minutes." She turned to Drew. "She loves her books."

Drew's eyes fixed on her. "I know what the camp meant to you. Some of my happiest childhood memories were made there too, but—it's more than that."

Janie swallowed hard. "What is it?"

"How could I live with myself if I hadn't signed? The land, the house—Riley's future. Mrs. Applegate wanted to provide you with a sense of security. She loved you, Janie."

Tears peppered her eyes for the loss of her friend and for the generous gift she'd left for her and Riley. "Thank you, Drew. I appreciate what you've done. I'll be honest— last year I went through a nasty divorce that has left me almost broke." Janie turned her focus down to the gravel parking lot. "I really didn't know how I would provide for Riley. I promise you, I'll do as much as I can on my own so this doesn't interfere with your job at the park."

Drew nodded. "But what about your ex-husband? Doesn't he have to pay you support or something?"

"Yes, he was ordered to pay both spousal and child support, but so far I haven't received anything." Janie examined her fingernails. "My lawyer has tried to garnish his wages, but my ex works as an independent contractor." At first she hesitated, not sure how much to share with Drew, but why not? She wasn't the one who was paid under the table. "Let's just say, he's good at hiding his income. It costs me money I don't have for my attorney to try to chase down the funds."

The couple continued across the lot. Drew's car horn sounded as he pushed the button to unlock his truck and pocketed his keys. He opened the passenger door and tossed his portfolio on the seat before turning to Janie. "We'll make it work. Since we're already in the first week of June, I don't think we can open for overnight guests by the Fourth, but a day camp would be doable."

Janie agreed. Most parents signed their children up for camp months in advance, but she had an idea. "I was thinking about that earlier, while you and Larry were talking. We'll meet the deadline of opening on the Fourth of July, but not for overnight guests, just a preview of what we'll have to offer. Then perhaps by late August, we—I mean, *I*—can host weekend overnights until the weather turns colder, if there's any interest."

A beat of silence ticked by before Drew responded. "I think that sounds like a good idea. If it would help, I'd be happy to assist you with your business plan."

Janie's feet shuffled, too embarrassed to admit to Drew that she didn't have the slightest idea what a business plan entailed. Tightness squeezed her chest. She didn't have a clue what she was doing, just like her ex always told her.

"Oh-kay then," Drew broke the uncomfortable silence. "We'll have to file all of the required paperwork for licensing by the state."

Janie looked up and shook her head. There was no point in trying to fool her old friend. "I hadn't even thought about that," she sighed.

"If you're going to eventually have overnight guests or any sort of cafeteria, you'll need licensing by the Department of Health," Drew added.

Oh boy. She was in way over her head. Her palms were slick with moisture. "I had no idea there was so much involved in running a camp. How did Mrs. Applegate do it alone for all of those years after her husband passed away?"

Janie had to admit, the terms of her friend's will stirred up a lot of emotions she'd tried desperately to keep contained. What if her ex-husband had been right about her being worthless and having no skills? Was she capable of operating a business on her own? But then she remembered Mrs. Applegate had known about the con-

trolling man Janie had married. Her friend knew exactly
what she'd been doing by leaving the camp to Janie. She
was providing an opportunity to prove her independence
and take control of her life. Janie couldn't help but wonder if this was also Mrs. Applegate's way of bringing her
and Drew back together again. With everything going
to the Alzheimer's Association if they didn't meet the
deadline, it seemed extreme. Did Mrs. Applegate plan
for more than just reigniting their friendship? Her friend
knew about her childhood crush. But Janie and Drew a
couple? There was no way that would ever happen. After
what Janie had experienced throughout her marriage,
giving her heart to another man wasn't in her future.

"How do you know so much about all of this?" she
asked.

Drew hesitated before he turned an empty stare in
her direction. "Let's just say once upon a time, I had a
dream of my own."

She wanted to ask Drew to expand on his comment.
She was curious about his dream, but it was best to hold
her peace and not pry into his business.

When Drew looked at her, the old familiar twinkle
in his eyes ignited goose bumps. For a second, she felt
calm. Drew could be trusted. She couldn't say that about
many men in her life—her ex had made certain of that
by constantly filling her head with demeaning comments. *You're not good enough. You'll never amount to
anything.* She forced his words from her mind.

"Thank you so much, Drew. At first I thought I had
everything under control…that I could do it all on my
own. How could I have been so naive? I'm trying to
understand why Mrs. Applegate would leave the prop-

erty to me." Janie squeezed her hand into a tight ball and released.

Drew turned to Janie and gently placed his hands on her arm, causing her stomach to flutter. "She understood how much it meant to you—that's why. I remember watching the two of you together. Like Larry said, she loved you like her own daughter. It only makes sense that she'd pass it along to you. She trusted you to keep her dream alive."

Janie sucked in a deep breath and exhaled. "Oh boy—that's a lot of pressure." What if the camp failed because of her? "I'm not sure I can do this, Drew." Her voice quivered.

"Nonsense. The Janie I remember did anything she put her mind to. Try not to worry so much and just take things one step at a time. I've got the day off on Saturday. Maybe we can meet in town for breakfast and work on your business plan."

Janie's mood had done a one-eighty since stepping outside of the lawyer's office. "Really? You'd do that for me?"

"It's not a big deal." Drew kicked some loose gravel under his shoe.

Janie considered his response. Perhaps it wasn't a big deal to him. After all, he wasn't exactly offering because he wanted to. He really had no choice if he hoped to fulfill Mrs. Applegate's wishes and claim his seventy-five acres. Still, she wanted to believe that even if the will hadn't laid out those terms, he'd volunteer to assist her in making the camp better than it had ever been. Growing up, that was the Drew she'd known and, if truth be told, loved. But that was a long time ago. Now she had to focus on her new business and keep her heart guarded.

Chapter Two

Drew sat at a corner bistro table in Huggamug Café. He lifted the oversize cup to his lips and inhaled the strong, but slightly bitter brew. Just the way he liked it. The shop buzzed with chatter from the typical Saturday crowd and the whirl of the bean grinder while patrons were coming and going to get their much-needed caffeine fix. The aroma of spicy cinnamon and freshly baked sugary treats teased his taste buds.

It had been another sleepless night. At five o'clock this morning, Drew gave up on sleep and left the comforts of his goose-down feather bed to watch the sun rise over the valley. It was his favorite way to begin his day and spend time alone with God. Drew had a lot of questions for Him. The first being why had He brought a vivacious seven-year-old into his life? Riley was the same age his daughter would be if he'd done his job and protected her. Didn't God know how painful this would be? And second, was he being forced to help Janie open her camp as punishment for not saving his wife and daughter? Or was this his second chance to save another family?

After downing his first cup of coffee, his head still spun like a merry-go-round. Since Janie and Riley had come back to town, he'd been unable to get them out of his mind. For a second, he'd thought of bolting from the café and heading back to the solitude of his cabin—away from people and from life. The bell over the door jingled, and he knew his opportunity to escape had passed. Drew's pulse tripped when he spotted Janie dressed in sky-blue running shorts, a white tank top and a white zip-up sweatshirt. Strange. Why would she be wearing a coat in early June? She'd worn a jacket when they'd met at the law firm, too. Maybe she was easily chilled by air-conditioning.

"Mr. Drew!" Riley called out in an excited tone. Her tennis shoes squeaked across the hardwood floor as she headed to his table. "Sorry we're late! Our car wouldn't start, so we had to walk." She flopped down in the padded red-and-white chair, blowing her hair away from her brown eyes. "It's kind of hot out there."

Drew loved Riley's energetic personality, but at the same time, it frightened him. He couldn't allow himself to get attached to this little girl. He turned his attention to the door and watched as Janie worked her way through the café to his table. Her striking appearance caused a few of the gentlemen at a nearby table to look up from their coffee cups. His teeth clenched. Wait—was he jealous? He shook off the feeling. This meeting was business, not pleasure.

"I'm sorry we kept you waiting on your day off." Janie's smile didn't quite reach her eyes. She took the empty chair closest to Drew. "I think my trusty twenty-year-old Honda might have driven its last mile yesterday."

"Yeah, this morning it made a terrible noise, like a

frog croaking," Riley added as she opened the menu the waitress had brought when Drew had first arrived. "Look, Mommy, the coffee cups are dancing." She pointed to the colorful cover and giggled.

Drew turned to Janie, catching a whiff of her perfume—sweet, like cotton candy. It reminded him of a trip to the boardwalk the summer before the accident. "Any idea what could be wrong?"

She shook her head. "I'm not sure. It's got a lot of mileage on it, but I'd just had it checked out by the mechanic before we made the trip from Maryland."

"I can take a look at it, if you'd like." He wasn't a trained mechanic, but he worked on his own cars enough to feel qualified to lend a hand.

Riley dropped the menu, her mouth hanging open. "You can fix cars, too? Man, Mr. Drew is like a superhero, isn't he, Mommy?"

His gut twisted as he lowered his gaze. The child was being nice. He was anything but a hero. "I've worked on cars here and there."

Janie tucked a strand of hair that had escaped from her ponytail behind her ear. "I've already imposed enough with my lack of business knowledge. I'll call my auto service, but thank you for the offer."

"You'll never get a mechanic to look at it over the weekend. Once we get a jump on your business plan for the camp, I'll drive you ladies home and take a look," Drew suggested. "It would be my pleasure."

"Mommy, can we take our food back to Uncle Nick's house? I miss Frankie." Riley stretched her arms out across the table.

Janie leaned forward. "Sweetie, don't lie on the table like that."

Drew raised a brow. "And who is Frankie?"

"He's my new puppy." Riley sat up straight and bounced in her chair. "We got him from my Uncle Nick. His dog Pebbles had three babies a couple of weeks before we moved here. I can't wait for you to meet him, Mr. Drew. He's so cute."

Janie scanned the room. "It is kind of noisy here. Maybe it would be best to get our breakfast to go and work at Nick's place."

Drew bit down on his lower lip. Working at the café, in a public place, kept things more businesslike and less personal, but he had to agree the crowd seemed quite rambunctious this morning. It would probably take twice as long to get anything accomplished. "That sounds like a good plan to me." Drew closed his portfolio and slid it inside his backpack.

"Janie Capello? Is that you?" a high-pitched voice called out from across the room. "Where in the world have you been?"

Drew glanced up and spotted Molly Morgan, the owner of the local bookstore, Bound to Please Reads. Her long, fiery red hair cascaded over her shoulders as she moved swiftly toward their table. After Molly had moved to Whispering Slopes when the two were in junior high school, they'd become best friends. Between their sleepovers and riding their bikes all around town, they'd been inseparable. It was obvious they hadn't kept in touch—but why?

"Molly!" Janie stood and embraced her old friend. "It's so great to see you."

The woman placed her hands on Janie's forearms. "I can't believe it's really you." They hugged again, this time holding on a little longer. "I've tried to find you for years. You never came back to visit, so I searched for you online. It was like you fell off the face of the earth. I thought everyone was on social media. Did you enter the witness protection program?" Molly barely stopped to catch a breath. "How are you? Who is this?" She glanced at Riley with a smile.

"I'm Riley and she's my mommy." Riley pointed at Janie. "My daddy didn't believe in social media."

Drew noticed Janie's cheeks redden. He was overwhelmed by all of Molly's rapid-fire questions. He imagined Janie was, too.

Janie half laughed. "Oh, Molly, you haven't changed a bit. I always thought you'd make a great prosecutor." She glanced at Drew and back to her friend. "Why don't you come over tomorrow morning for breakfast so we can catch up?"

"That sounds great. I can come over after church." She tugged on her purse strap. "Better yet, how about I pick up you and Riley and we can all go to service together? It will be just like old times. Remember when we'd ride our bikes to the Sunday school?" Molly laughed.

"My daddy didn't believe in church, either."

"Riley!"

Drew watched Janie's jaw tighten while she pulled on the sleeve of her jacket. Growing up, her family always went to church. She was the reason he started attending.

Janie focused her attention back on Molly. "I'm sorry—services won't be possible for us tomorrow, but if you want to swing by afterward, I can fix us some lunch."

"Yeah, Daddy wouldn't want me to go," Riley added.

"Enough, Riley. We're going to be busy in the morning. We have a lot to do to get the camp ready to reopen." Exhaling an annoyed breath, she turned her attention away from her daughter and back to her friend, her eyes skimming over Drew. "Come by Nick's house anytime, Molly. That's where we're staying."

The two friends hugged again and said their good-byes until tomorrow. Drew considered Janie's reaction to Molly's invitation. Why was she so opposed to going to church? Her ex-husband didn't believe in church? The Janie he remembered wouldn't marry someone without a strong faith in God. A weight grew heavy on his heart. Something just didn't add up.

As Drew guided his oversize truck up Nick's drive-way all Janie could think about was whether or not the kitchen sink was full of last night's dinner dishes. Her ex-husband had always been meticulous about cleaning, almost to the point of obsessive. Janie found pleasure in running the house the way she wanted. She had to admit, leaving an occasional bowl or plate in the sink gave her a twinge of satisfaction.

"Well, if you're going to house-sit in the Valley, this is the place to do it," Drew stated as he put the vehicle into Park and unfastened his seat belt. "The view here is incredible."

"There's butterflies everywhere, too!" Riley added from the backseat as she unhooked her belt.

Janie glanced out the window at the one-story ranch. She had to agree with Drew. From the moment they'd arrived in the quaint neighborhood, she'd realized it would make a comfortable, yet temporary home for her and Riley. It was a perfect refuge from her violent past. The mountain laurel was in full bloom and the sweet aroma of honeysuckle gave her a peaceful feeling. It was a far cry from their home in Maryland.

"I agree. Even though we're house-sitting for Nick, it feels like home."

"If you'd like, once you get the keys to Mrs. Applegate's—I mean, your new house, I can go over there with you to see what kind of repairs it might need."

Janie's heart warmed. "That's really a generous offer, Drew." She was anxious to start making a permanent home for her and Riley. She still hadn't gotten over the shock that she was actually going to be a homeowner. When Janie woke up the morning after meeting with the attorney, she'd been afraid it had all been a dream. "I'm excited to see the place."

Drew stepped down from the vehicle. "Mary always kept an immaculate home, so I don't expect too much in the way of repairs. Of course, you might want to do some upgrades. I'm pretty good when it comes to updating kitchens, bathrooms—most every room in the house."

"See, Mommy," Riley called out as she jumped from the truck. "I told you Mr. Drew can do anything." Her daughter grinned. "It's going to be so much fun. Since I don't start school until the end of August, I can help, too." She stopped quickly and turned to Drew. "I'm really happy that lady said you have to help us, Mr. Drew." She motioned for him to bend over and when he complied, she whispered in his ear.

"Hey—no secrets, you two." Janie waved a finger in the air. "What were you telling him, Riley?"

The little girl giggled. She briefly placed her hand over her mouth then jerked it away. "I told him that I don't think you know anything about starting a camp, but he probably does since he's out in the woods a lot."

"Funny girl." Janie grabbed the bag of food resting

on the backseat. "I hope everyone is hungry. We've got enough food here to feed the entire town."

"Let's hurry up and go inside," Riley called out as she reached for Drew's hand. "I can't wait for you to meet Frankie."

Janie observed the two with reservations. The last thing she wanted was for her daughter to get attached to Drew. But what about her? Growing up, they'd been the best of friends, but she'd had a secret crush on him. She needed to keep her feelings in check. Drew was simply honoring Mrs. Applegate's wishes to help with the camp, so he could take control of his portion of the land. Nothing more. But the will didn't state he had to help get her and Riley settled into their new home or fix her car. Sliding the key into the lock, she pushed the front door open. When it came to Drew Brenner, she'd need to keep her guard up. After years in an abusive marriage, how could she trust any man again?

As soon as the door opened, the rambunctious jet-black puppy scurried toward them, his toenails skidding across the hardwood floor. "Hey, Frankie." Drew kneeled and rubbed the dog's head. "A lab. They're the best."

Frankie licked Drew's hand. It was obvious they'd formed an immediate bond. What was it about a man and a dog?

"He likes you, Mr. Drew. He's small now, but he'll get really big. Right, Mommy?"

Janie rolled her eyes at Drew. "Yes…unfortunately. It's a good thing we'll be living on the farm. He'll have plenty of room to get outside." She could only imagine how much it would cost to feed Frankie. He was already eating like a horse. "Thankfully, Pebbles is staying with some of Nick and Joy's friends. I don't think I could handle two dogs."

Janie headed toward the kitchen while Drew and her daughter shadowed behind. She breathed a sigh of relief when she spotted the sink clear of dinner dishes. "I'll get the food ready for us." She placed the bag containing their breakfast on the countertop before turning to her daughter. "Why don't you take Frankie outside to burn off a little energy?"

"Okay. You come too, Mr. Drew. I'll show you the tree house. Uncle Nick built it for my cousins. It's so cool!"

Seeing her daughter so happy warmed Janie's heart. Only a week ago, Riley had cried half the drive from Maryland to Whispering Slopes. She'd been angry at her mother for taking her away from her friends and her father. Janie didn't have the heart to tell her that her father had no desire to seek any visitation rights. His loss. She couldn't help but wonder whether she would have put up a fight if he had tried to exercise his legal right. She'd never seen him so much as raise his voice to his daughter. Perhaps that's why he didn't seek visitation. Maybe he didn't trust himself. Whatever his reasons had been, she was grateful not to have contact with him, but she couldn't help but wonder about the long-term effects on her daughter. Would she grow up feeling abandoned? She forced the thoughts from her mind, refusing to allow them to cloud the present.

Janie busied herself making a fresh pot of coffee and warming up the food they'd brought from the café. She found comfort being in the kitchen, even if it wasn't her own. Within minutes the room smelled of crispy bacon and garlic home-fried potatoes. She carefully placed the breakfast on the table and headed toward the back door to call Drew and Riley inside for the meal. She hesitated for a moment as she peered out the window, taking notice of the sadness in Drew's eyes. He watched Riley turning somersaults in the green fescue as she laughed with each turn of her small body. When he wiped his left eye with the back of his hand, Janie loosened her fingers from the doorknob. Why was he having this reaction to her daughter? His dejected posture was troublesome.

Forty minutes later, with everyone's plate practically licked clean, Drew stood and reached for Janie's breakfast dish. "Let me get these."

She rested her hand on his as she pushed her chair away from the table. "You don't have to do that. I'll take care of it." Stuffed to the gills after the enormous Western omelet and hash browns, she needed to move.

Drew ignored her words and carried the dishes to the sink.

"Mommy, can I go next door to see if Leslie can play?" Riley asked, sitting on the floor with her face nuzzled into the top of Frankie's head.

Janie lifted her daughter's plate from the table and crossed to the sink where Drew was busy loading the dishwasher. "Let me text Leslie's mother and see if she wants to come over. You two can play in the tree house."

Since the move, Janie's protective instincts had gone into overdrive. She struggled with letting her daughter out of arm's reach. She liked the family next door. When they'd moved into the house, Janie had been thrilled to learn there was a little girl living next door who was the same age as Riley. They seemed like good people, but she just felt more at ease with Riley playing where she could keep a close eye on her.

"Okay. Thanks, Mommy. I'll be out back with Frankie." Riley skipped outside with her puppy on her heels. The screen door closed with a bang.

"I need to do something with that door. She goes in and out all day. The constant slamming is driving me bananas." Janie grabbed her phone off the granite countertop and shot a quick text to Leslie's mother.

"I can fix the door for you—if you'd like."

A smile tugged on Janie's lips. "You like to repair things, don't you?"

Their eyes spent a second too long fixated on each other. Drew's cheeks flushed.

Janie's phone beeped an immediate reply to her text confirming the playdate. She placed the device on the counter and stepped to the sink. "If you keep this up, I think I'll need to invite you over more often." Every breakfast dish had been cleaned and Drew was busy wiping down the counters, not leaving a single crumb behind. And now he was offering his services for home repairs. A feeling of comfort crept in, but she shook it off. When it came to men, her sense of judgment couldn't be trusted, even if it was her old friend Drew.

"I guess we can work at the table, if that's okay with you."

"That sounds good." Drew dried his hands then carefully folded the dish towel before heading toward his backpack he'd stowed in the corner earlier.

They settled into their chairs and Janie watched as Drew removed some files from the canvas bag. "I did some research on business plans geared toward camps." He opened a folder and removed the large binder clip. Janie watched his strong hand as he flipped through some pages—a lot of pages.

"Wow, you're not kidding. I think you've gone above and beyond." A twinge of guilt settled when she noticed his perfectly handwritten notes along with articles he'd printed from the internet.

"Maybe Mrs. Applegate should have left the property to you." Her shoulders slumped. Was she getting in over her head?

"Nonsense. She left it in capable hands. Besides, I'm just a natural researcher. Give me a topic and I'll learn everything about it in a twenty-four-hour period."

Janie's brow arched in response. "I don't remember you being that way in school." She playfully nudged him with her elbow and winked. "In fact, I seem to recall a big history assignment where we were paired together during our freshman year. You stood me up in the library each time we were scheduled to meet."

Drew turned with an arched brow. "Who? Me?"

"Yes—you! I ended up doing the entire paper by myself even though both of our names were on it." In those days she'd had such a crush on him, so she'd let it slide.

"Yeah, that wasn't too cool, was it? I'm sorry. I was so absorbed with football." He rested his hands on the pile of paperwork. "I should have focused more on school, but when I made varsity my first year in high school, I actually thought I had a chance to play for the pros after graduation."

"Why didn't you?" Janie always believed he was good enough. She remembered some big-name colleges were interested in him.

Drew shook his head. "After my dad passed away during our senior year, I couldn't imagine leaving my mom and going away to school. Losing him was really tough on her. I completed basic EMT training and became certified."

"You're a paramedic, too?"

His voice dropped. "Not anymore."

Losing his father had to have been difficult on him. Janie remembered how they used to spend hours in the yard tossing the football. "I was so sorry to hear about your father, Drew. I wish I'd been here." She was familiar with the pain of losing a parent. Despite rounds of rehab, her mother had OD'd during Janie's senior year of high school, two years after they'd left Whispering Slopes. Sadly, her father had since passed on, too. "How is your mother now?" Janie had always loved Drew's mother. Like Mrs. Applegate, she'd stepped up to the plate when her own mother had slipped further into her addiction.

"She's good. A few years ago, she decided to move to Florida to live with her older sister. My aunt's health wasn't good, so it made sense. It gave my mother a fresh start."

"Do you regret not going away to college?" As soon as the question escaped her lips, she wanted to take it back. This wasn't any of her business.

Drew turned his attention back to the files in front of him. "I'd rather not talk about the past. We have a lot of work to do to get your camp up and running. But first, let me go take a look at your car."

Janie watched as Drew neatly arranged the research into a perfect pile before walking out to the garage. How different would her life be if her family hadn't moved away? But she couldn't continue to dwell on her past and all of the mistakes she had made. She needed to let go and move on. Looking down at her covered arms, she tugged on the long sleeves knowing that was easier said than done.

Chapter Three

Drew's body jerked and his eyes shot wide-open. A cold sweat plastered his hair to the cotton sheet. His right hand trembled while he reached for the bottle of water on the oak nightstand. The nightmare that had him wide-awake at three-thirty Sunday morning was hazy. The accident was clear, but the events that followed were jumbled and blurred. His wife, Lori, had walked away unscathed. Only it wasn't Lori in the dream…it was Janie. She'd stood silent on the edge of the road watching the car burn, while Drew struggled to open the back door of the vehicle—only to reveal a tree house in the backseat instead of his daughter.

He drained the bottle and swung his legs over the side of his mattress, the hardwood floor cool to his feet. He knew the drill. Sleep wouldn't come again anytime soon. As he padded down the hall of his secluded cabin, the light from the full moon put a spotlight on the last photograph taken with his family. He approached the sofa table and picked up the frame. His legs no longer able to hold him upright, he collapsed on the couch.

Tears dotted his eyelashes as he studied the smiles. Heidi's first ballet recital. Drew wiped his eyes. She'd been so happy when he'd presented her with her first bouquet of roses. *Why, God? Why didn't you take me instead of my family? It should have been me. I don't know how to live without them.*

A half an hour later, Drew peeled his body off the sofa and carefully returned the picture to its proper place. Time spent with Janie and her daughter had no doubt triggered the nightmare. It had been over a year since he'd last dreamed about his family, but that had been a happy one. It was a picturesque day and he'd taken his family on a picnic. They'd run through the open meadow and picked wildflowers. A perfect afternoon, even if it was only a dream.

Drew headed to the spare bedroom. When he'd moved in two years ago, he'd placed the small pine desk by the window so he could enjoy the scenic view of the Blue Ridge Mountains. He fired up his laptop. The sooner he could get Janie's camp up and running the better. They'd gotten a lot accomplished yesterday. With Janie's help, Drew had written up a business plan and had made a list of all the licensing she'd need to operate the camp legally. He'd made a promise he'd be available if she had any questions or problems.

Today he planned to hit the early church service, work his half-day shift and then head over to the Applegate property to check out the existing structures. The camp had been in operation up until Mrs. Applegate started to have some health problems, so he didn't anticipate too much work would need to be done to get it ready to open—at least he hoped not.

* * *

That afternoon as Drew traveled down the gravel road on the Applegate property, he admired the rolling farmland. Growing up, he'd spent so much time here. His heart warmed at the thought of owning a piece of the land where so many wonderful childhood memories had been created. He paused at the realization that most of those great times had included Janie.

A trail of dust chased the back end of the truck. The gravel crunched under the weight of the tires. As he approached the old barn where most of the farm equipment used to be stored, Drew thought it might be nice to get a couple of goats and some other animals so the children could learn how to care for them, but really that would be up to Janie. Even a pig or two would be nice for Riley. He pulled his truck alongside the structure and was surprised to see Janie's car parked around back. The vehicle was up and running once again. Mission accomplished. He hopped out of his truck and took in a lungful of fresh mountain air, wishing he could bottle it.

"Mr. Drew!"

He jumped at the sound of the high-pitched voice coming from inside of the barn.

"What are you doing here?" Riley darted toward him at top speed.

"I thought I'd check things out a bit." The door to the barn creaked and Janie appeared. Drew sucked down a breath in an attempt to slow his heartbeat. It didn't work. Dressed in white shorts with her hair pulled back in a ponytail, she reminded him of that young girl he'd had a secret crush on at camp. His eyes traveled to her arms that were once again covered with a long-sleeved sweatshirt. The air was still with a touch of humidity and the midday sun was warm. With temperatures approaching the middle eighties, why a sweatshirt?

"I guess we both had the same idea. By the way, thanks again for fixing my car. She's running great." Janie pointed toward the vehicle.

Drew nodded as she moved toward him carrying a spiral notebook and a fluorescent green pen. "I was up most of the night worrying about what would need to be repaired before we could open." She slipped the end of the pen between her pink lips as she looked back at the barn.

Drew took notice of the word *we*. Had Janie misunderstood the terms laid out in the will and thought they'd be running the camp together? That could never happen. "So did you see anything that needs work?"

Her smile slipped from her lips. "Unfortunately, it looks like some mice have taken up residency in a couple of the cabins." Her face scrunched up.

"Well, that should be an easy fix. Once I get rid of those critters, I'll use some sealing foam. Hopefully, that will keep them out." He could handle a few mice… better than snakes.

She pulled the sleeves of her sweatshirt down over her hands. "That might be simple, but I don't think fixing the hole in the roof will be that easy, though."

"What roof?"

Janie turned around and pointed. "The barn."

That didn't sound good, but hopefully not a major repair. "Did you see anything else?"

When she opened her notebook and flipped some pages, he prepared himself for the worst.

As Janie rattled off the list of repairs she had recorded, Drew realized these easy fixes might not be simple after all.

"I guess I'll need to make a copy, so I can prioritize the work." He always liked to tackle the more difficult jobs first. Sadly, he had failed at the most important job—protecting his family.

"Oh, I wrote out two lists. The other copy is here." She stepped closer and a delightful smell of lavender drifted toward his nose. Janie licked her index finger and flipped over a few pages. "I figured I'd take care of the jobs that don't require too much muscle or the use of anything mechanical."

He laughed, recalling freshman shop class in high school. "That sounds like a good plan. Remember the handsaw? I didn't know metal could bend like that."

Janie's eyes popped and she playfully bumped her shoulder against his. "What do you mean? I got a good grade on that project."

"If I recall, it was a C."

She rolled her eyes. "It was a C-plus, mister."

The couple laughed as they recalled the happy memory.

"I can do some stuff too, Mr. Drew." Riley looked up from the dandelions she'd been picking.

Drew took another look at the to-do list before turning to Riley. "Of course you can—you'll be my assistant." He winked as Riley did a quick fist pump.

Yesterday, when he and Janie had prepared the business plan, they'd also worked on their timeline. They had a little over three weeks. He rubbed his hand across his unshaven chin. They could never reach that goal. There weren't enough hours in the day after he patrolled the forest. "Look, this is going to take longer than I thought. Tomorrow, I'm going to talk to my supervisor about taking some time off from the day job."

A worried expression washed over Janie's face. "Oh

no, I'll just hire someone to do all of the repairs. I can't ask you to use your vacation time for me."

"You didn't. I'm offering. Besides, I haven't taken leave since I started my job early last year. Plus, there are some new guys who are always looking to pick up extra shifts." He turned his eyes in her direction and the smile that lit up her face told him he was doing the right thing, but was he risking his heart in the process?

"Here, Mommy." Riley pushed herself off the ground and handed her mother a cluster of yellow flowers.

"Aw, thank you, sweetie." Janie accepted the gift with a smile.

Drew observed the affection between mother and daughter and one thought kept rattling around in his brain. He had to do this for them. But when his gaze connected with Janie's exquisite beauty, he couldn't help but wonder how he could keep the arrangement with her strictly professional and protect his heart as he spent time with a sweet little girl who was a constant reminder of his own child.

"Mommy." Holding Frankie on her lap, Riley wiggled in the car seat in the back of the car as they headed to the farm on Monday morning.

Easing her foot off the accelerator as the light signal changed to red, Janie turned around to the sound of her daughter's sweet voice. Her heart warmed at the sight of her little girl with her face nuzzled against Frankie. A gift from God. And the only good that came from a disastrous marriage. "Yes, sweetie?"

"How come Daddy didn't want to share me with you?"

The question rattled Janie's foundation. Riley didn't

deserve this. She shouldn't have to question her father's love for her. "What do you mean?"

The child lifted her head away from the dog. "Before we left Maryland, Rachel said when parents get a divorce they share the kids." She paused and glanced out the car window. "I forget what she called it."

Janie hadn't, but her ex-husband never mentioned the words while the divorce papers were being drawn up by the attorneys. "They share custody, sweetie."

"Yeah, that's it. Why didn't you and Daddy do that? Doesn't he love me anymore?" Riley's face went back into the animal's fur.

Janie turned her attention back to the road the moment the light turned green. Her heart crumbled. How could she respond when she really didn't know the answer herself? Janie couldn't help but think the reason Riley's father had walked away from his daughter was to hurt her mother one last time. He'd never be able to lay another hand on his wife, but he could continue to cause pain by making Janie watch her daughter question his love.

Janie's stomach tightened as she glanced at her hands clutching the steering wheel of her SUV. Although her ring finger was now bare, the scars remained. How could she have been so wrong about the man she thought she'd grow old with?

"I think your father is confused about a lot of things." Janie reached behind and squeezed her daughter's hand, firmly holding the wheel with the other.

"Maybe God could help him? Back home, my friend Suzanne and her family used to go to church and pray for stuff. Do you think that's possible, Mommy?"

Riley's loaded question was something Janie had prayed for throughout her marriage. She'd tried to convince her ex to come to church and speak with their pastor, but he'd refused. "I think the best thing we can do is pray for your father." After all of the pain, both physical and verbal, that Janie had endured, praying for this man had not been easy, but it was the only way she'd have peace in her life. She needed to forgive, but she struggled with doing so when it came to Randy.

Mother and daughter drove in silence for several minutes. "Maybe Mr. Drew would want to be my daddy. Do you think he would?" Riley asked as she leaned forward toward Janie.

Yesterday, when Molly had come by for lunch, she'd questioned Janie about Drew. In passing, Molly had mentioned how difficult the past couple of years had been for him, but she hadn't gone into any details. She'd gotten teary eyed and said it would be best if she heard it from Drew.

"Do you?" Riley waited for an answer.

After her divorce, Janie's wedding ring had been pawned for much-needed cash, but the pain of those years wasn't so easily discarded. When it came to men and relationships, could she ever trust her judgment again? What would Drew think about what was underneath the material that covered her arms and concealed the shame?

"Honey, we need to keep our focus on getting the camp up and running by the Fourth of July. Mr. Drew is simply helping us in order to get his portion of the land left to him by Mrs. Applegate."

"But I like him. I think he'd make a great daddy."

Janie agreed with her daughter. She also thought Drew would be a loving and devoted husband. But she'd believed that once about her first husband and look how that turned out. Perhaps one day Drew would have a family of his own, but definitely not with her.

After pulling in to the farm, Janie got Riley and Frankie out of the car, then headed to the barn. Standing inside the barn with her hands on her hips, she watched the sun stream through the gigantic hole in the roof. How would she ever meet the deadline? There seemed to be so many things in need of repair. She'd have to focus on one task at a time and try not to look at the big picture. Easier said than done.

Outside, Frankie barked at the rumbling engine approaching. Janie went to investigate. When she spotted Drew's truck, her shoulders relaxed. Of course it was him.

"Mommy! Mr. Drew is here. He's here!" Riley jumped up and down.

Watching the vehicle move closer, Janie placed her hand to the side of her face. Riley's excited tone concerned her. But what could she do? Her daughter needed a home and the only way to make that happen was to work with Drew.

"Good morning, ladies." Drew stepped down from the truck. Dressed in jeans, a white T-shirt that magnified his large biceps and a ball cap, he appeared ready to get to work. He strolled to the passenger-side door and removed a large toolbox.

Janie watched as Riley ran to him. When her daughter's arms wrapped around his legs, Janie melted just a bit.

"We've been waiting for you, Mr. Drew. Mommy's been staring at that big hole in the roof," the child explained.

"She has?" Drew walked toward the barn. "Well, I plan to take care of that this morning. I've got Earl

Moore dropping off some wood within the hour. He'll be bringing his two-man crew to help us."

The tension eased in Janie's body. She looked up toward the cloud-flecked sky. *Thank You, God.*

A noise came from the barn and Frankie took off running.

"Frankie! Wait for me," Riley chased the dog through the grassy meadow. "Ouch—my arm!" she cried out.

Janie turned as her daughter fell to the ground and burst into tears. In a split second she was kneeling next to Riley. Drew followed.

"What is it, sweetie?" Janie examined the child's arm then turned to Drew. "It's swelling."

Drew observed the injury. "She must have gotten stung by a bee. There're a lot of yellow jackets this time of the year."

As the adults tried to calm Riley, her arm grew more red and swollen.

"It really hurts, Mommy. My throat feels funny, too," she cried.

Janie's eyes widened. "What does it feel like?"

Riley struggled with the words. "I can't breathe."

Drew scooped up the child and sprung to his feet. "She's having an allergic reaction to the sting." He sprinted toward his truck with Riley whimpering in his arms. "Hurry! We have to get her to the hospital— now! I'll call and let them know we're on our way. Grab Frankie and her booster seat!"

Janie gasped and covered her mouth. Grabbing the dog, then racing to her car for Riley's seat, Janie willed her feet to move faster while fearful thoughts swirled in her head. *God, please help her. She's all I have.* What if they didn't get her help in time?

Chapter Four

The ten-minute drive to Shenandoah Memorial seemed endless. Threatening storm clouds formed overhead, peppering the windshield with fat drops of rain. Drew's truck hugged the sharp curves of the mountain road. His hands gripped firmly to the steering wheel. Precious cargo was on board. He had to keep them safe. He couldn't fail, again. For a split second, back at the farm, Drew questioned whether they should have called 911, but he was confident he could get Riley to the hospital faster. During a quick call to the hospital's front desk explaining the emergency, the nurse assured him a gurney would be ready when they arrived.

"It seems like it's taking forever," Janie cried out from the backseat while gently rubbing Riley's forehead.

The little girl coughed and released a slight whimper.

"We're almost there." Drew silently prayed he would be given a second chance. He hadn't been able to save his wife and his daughter. He wouldn't allow Riley to suffer the same fate.

A few minutes later his shoulders loosened when he

spotted the glowing red lights of the emergency-room entrance. He guided the vehicle up to the curb and hit the horn. Within seconds, two orderlies pushing a gurney raced through the doors. Time was of the essence when dealing with an allergic reaction to a bee sting.

Janie bolted from the truck as one of the two men carefully lifted Riley out of the car seat and placed her on the gurney.

"Mommy," Riley whispered, then coughed.

"You go with them. I'll park and be right inside," Drew called out to Janie through the open window.

Moments later Drew rushed through the doors and spotted Janie talking with Nell, the head nurse. The woman rubbed Janie's arm in an attempt to console her.

"Is she with the doctor?" Drew's eyes flitted between the two women.

"They took her back immediately. I can see her as soon as they move her into a room." Janie collapsed in the brown vinyl chair, covered her eyes and wept.

"What is it, Nell?" Drew asked while outside thunder roared like a lion in captivity.

The nurse stepped in closer. "It appears Riley has gone into anaphylactic shock. I told Janie the doctor has a lot of experience with these types of reactions, so Riley is in good hands." Nell reached for Janie's hand. "I'll go find out how she's doing."

Janie looked up, her eyes soaked with tears. "Thank you."

Nell scurried down the hall.

Drew pulled a chair beside Janie. "I'm so sorry." If he'd called the ambulance the paramedics could have started treatment when they arrived at the farm. Had he made the wrong decision by bringing Riley to the hospital himself? "I shouldn't have driven her."

"You did what you thought was best. I don't think either one of us imagined this would happen."

How could he not? He'd worked as a paramedic and witnessed dozens of reactions to bee stings. "I should have taken extra precaution."

"Please, don't blame yourself, Drew. You got us here in record time. I don't think the ambulance could have arrived at the farm any faster."

Drew wasn't convinced. *Please, God, let Riley be okay.*

The room buzzed with excitement. Janie and Drew waited patiently for an update from the doctor. Through the chatter, Drew learned a large family was anticipating the birth of twins. His mind flooded with memories of the birth of his daughter. At first he wasn't sure if he could handle being in the delivery room with Lori, but in the end, he watched Heidi enter the world. It had been the happiest day of his life. Never in his wildest dreams would he have imagined that only seven brief years later, he'd watch her leave this earth. A cold chill whished through his body as he tried to obliterate the horrible day from his thoughts.

After what seemed like an eternity, the doors to the ER swished open and Dr. Macgregor approached the waiting room.

Janie sprung from the chair. "How is Riley, doctor?"

Drew stood and rested his hand on Janie's back. She flinched, so he pulled away.

The doctor punched a few keys on his tablet before addressing Janie. "You can relax. She's going to be fine. She's resting now, but I'd like to keep her overnight, just as a precaution."

"Can I stay with her? We've never spent a night apart from each other." Janie tugged on the sleeve of her jacket.

"Of course you can. I've given Riley some medication to help her sleep. Understandably, she was quite anxious from the incident."

Janie looked up at the doctor. "How can I prevent this from happening again?"

"Obviously, there is no guarantee that Riley will never be stung by a bee again, so you'll both need to carry an EpiPen Jr."

Janie swiped her hand across her brow. "I've heard of that, but I don't really know what it is."

Dr. Macgregor tapped a few keystrokes and turned the screen toward Janie. "This is what it looks like. It's an injection containing epinephrine."

"What exactly is that?" Janie asked.

"It's a chemical that narrows the blood vessels and opens airways in the lungs. The effects can reverse severely low blood pressure, wheezing, skin itching, hives and other symptoms of an allergic reaction."

Drew considered Janie as she listened to the doctor's explanation and studied the screen.

"Will Riley be able to use it on her own? She's so young."

"Don't worry—we'll show her how to use it, but it's important she carry it with her everywhere. Often when a person has a reaction to a sting, the intensity can get worse with each sting."

Drew admired the doctor's honesty. It was important for Janie to know these types of allergic reactions can be dangerous. He'd seen it many times.

"When can I go back there? I want to see for myself that she's okay." Janie yanked each of her sleeves.

Dr. Macgregor removed his glasses and pocketed them inside his white coat. "I can take you to her now, if you'd like?"

"Oh yes, please." Janie's voice lifted for the first time since they'd arrived at the hospital. She turned to Drew. "Do you want to come with me?"

"No, you go ahead. If you're staying the night, I'll go on and head home."

Janie stepped closer to Drew. "Thank you for getting Riley to the hospital in time. You made the right decision not waiting for the ambulance." She gave him a quick hug. "I don't even want to think about what could have happened."

"Then don't. You heard the doctor. Riley is going to be fine. Now we know how to respond if she's stung again. We'll be prepared…I mean, you'll be prepared."

"You're right." Janie turned and headed down the hallway with the doctor.

"Janie?" Drew called out. She turned with a slight smile. "Since you don't have a car here, I'll come by in the morning and pick up you and Riley. I'll take Frankie home with me tonight."

Janie nodded and hurried down the hall. Soon she'd be reunited with her daughter.

A twinge of jealousy tugged at Drew. He longed for a reunion with his own family. His shoulders slumped as he headed for the door. Outside, the sun sank behind the mountains as the cicadas sounded like a chorus. He popped the lock on his truck and settled against the cool leather seat. Leaning forward, he rested his forehead against the steering wheel.

The events of the day had left him physically and emotionally drained. Seeing Riley suffer had ignited a firestorm of memories he'd tried so hard to keep locked away over the past two years. Had he made a mistake signing the papers at the attorney's office? Was he ready to give up his life of solitude for a constant reminder of what could have been? A life spent providing for a family, growing old with your partner. If only he'd been able to save the two people who'd mattered most in the world—but he didn't.

Getting the camp ready would make the weeks ahead difficult, but he needed to ensure Janie and Riley had a roof over their heads and money to live a comfortable life. The pain would be worth it. He turned the key to head home to his empty cabin. Alone.

"Mommy? Are you here?"

Tuesday morning, Riley's soft voice pulled Janie from a fitful night of rest. She jumped to her feet, then rushed to her daughter's bedside. Her back hitched from the hard hospital chair. "Yes, sweetie, I'm here." She brushed her hand across Riley's forehead.

"Where am I?" The young girl raised her bare arm and examined the IV. "Where's Mr. Drew? I remember him carrying me."

Outside in the hallway the intercom paged a doctor to examination room four. "We're at the hospital, baby. You got stung by a bee yesterday. Do you remember?"

Janie watched as her daughter glanced at the spot where she'd been stung. "Yeah, it still hurts a little. How can something so tiny hurt so much?" Riley crinkled her brow. "Where's Mr. Drew?"

"He'll be here to pick us up once the doctor says it's

okay for you to go home." Janie found Riley's fixation on Drew a bit concerning.

"Why does the doctor have to tell me I can leave?"

"You had an allergic reaction to the bee sting. Remember how you felt?"

Riley nodded. "It felt like there was no air for me to breathe."

Janie's stomach twisted. What she wouldn't give to trade places with her little girl. "That feeling you had isn't normal. Most people who get stung just have a little pain for a while."

"It definitely didn't hurt a little. It hurt a lot."

"I know it did, sweetie. Why don't you try to get a little more rest," Janie suggested.

"I'd rather sleep in my own bed. Can we go home now?"

Janie was looking forward to a nap in her own bed, too, but it would be a while before Riley would be released. "Let's wait for the doctor. He's going to give you something in case you're ever stung again, so you don't have a reaction like you did."

"Oh, that pen thing?"

"It's called an EpiPen. How do you know about that?" Her daughter was growing up faster than she'd like.

Riley pushed herself up a little. "Back in Maryland, my friend Suzanne had one. They're kind of cool."

Janie had forgotten all about Suzanne and her severe peanut allergy. She was relieved to know Riley was okay with having to carry one with her. "I didn't remember that."

"I watched her use it once when Teddy Forbes had

shared some cookies with her. He didn't know they had peanuts in them. It didn't look hard."

"Well, let's just pray you'll never have to use the pen, but we need to wait for the doctor to demonstrate for us. In the meantime, do you want me to run down to the cafeteria and get us some breakfast?"

Riley squirmed under the covers. "Yes, please. I'll have toast with grape jelly and juice, too."

Janie walked over to her makeshift bed and grabbed her purse off the nearby table. "Why don't you close your eyes for a while and get a little more rest."

"Okay, Mommy."

She waited and watched as Riley drifted off to sleep. Her eyelids fluttered. Janie headed out the door toward the cafeteria.

"Janie!"

Surprised, she spun around and spotted Drew. Her insides vibrated as he approached. He was dressed in relaxed jeans and a dark leather jacket that accentuated his muscular build. Next to him she felt like a load of clothes forgotten in the washing machine. She smoothed her hair, even though it wouldn't do much good. What she needed was a shower.

"Hey, how's the munchkin doing?" His smile lit up his face.

Janie had to admit, apart from seeing Riley this morning the sight of Drew had been the highlight of her time spent in the hospital.

"She's doing well. I asked her to try to rest while I get us some breakfast. Would you like to join me?"

Drew rubbed his stomach. "I was hoping you'd ask. I skipped breakfast, so I'm famished."

They headed down the corridor. Nurses padded from

room to room. Inside the cafeteria, the aroma of strong-brewed coffee filled the air.

"That's exactly what I need."

Drew turned to Janie. "What's that?"

"Gallons of strong coffee…black. I never realized how hard it is to sleep sitting up." Janie rubbed the back of her neck.

"Why don't you grab a table and I'll get your caffeine fix. We can discuss the repairs on the barn before we get our breakfast," Drew suggested.

Janie had planned on grabbing the food to go, but maybe it was best if she let Riley rest a little longer. "That sounds like a good idea."

Minutes later Drew approached the table with two steaming cups of brew. He set down the beverages and took a seat. "I wanted to give you an update. After we rushed to the hospital yesterday, Earl Moore and his crew came by with the cedar and started work on the barn."

Janie's shoulders relaxed, and she was thrilled to hear they weren't losing time due to Riley's stay in the hospital. "That's wonderful, Drew. How much do I owe them?"

Drew shook his head. "Don't worry about that now, in Whispering Slopes people do for one another—that's the way it's always been. They'll get paid through the estate. Larry will take care of it."

Janie leaned back against the chair and admired the view outside. The arched, floor-to-ceiling window provided a breathtaking view of the mountains. "I almost forgot how beautiful it is here. I guess as kids we don't appreciate it as much." She took a slow sip of her brew. "I can see why you decided to become a ranger. Your office, so to speak, is so peaceful."

Drew turned his attention to the towering mountain range and exhaled. "The trails winding through the Blue Ridge saved my life."

Janie studied Drew's pained expression. "How so?" Something had happened in his past—Molly had alluded to that—but she didn't want to pry into his personal life. Still, she was curious as to why he'd leave his job working as a paramedic.

Drew sat up a little straighter in his chair. His eyes held pain. "I've spent the past two years clawing my way through a valley of darkness I'd never wish on my worst enemy." He paused as crinkle lines formed around his eyes. "When I couldn't save my own family, I lost all confidence and hope to save others. That's why I left my job as a paramedic."

Janie's breath slowed, almost stopping. "You have a family?"

Drew's focus remained glued on his coffee cup as though the now-tepid brew held answers he'd been searching for. Then he lifted his head and brushed the moisture from his lashes. "No. I had a family, Janie."

Chapter Five

Drew took a long pull on his bottle of water. He and Skip Keller, a paramedic and friend, had been hard at work on the roof of the barn since sunrise. Earl and his guys were assisting Mrs. Whipple with her deck expansion today, so Skip had insisted on helping Drew. Growing up, he'd also loved to attend the Applegates' camp. Skip had been Drew's closest friend and was there for him at the lowest point in his life.

"It's going to be a steamer." Skip wiped the sweat from his brow.

Visitors usually escaped to the mountains for a break from the heat and humidity, but on this Thursday morning there was no way to avoid it. "Yeah, the local weatherman said we'd be in the high eighties today. Thankfully, we should have a break by the end of the week," Drew stated.

Skip picked up his water and took a swig before glancing toward the sky. "Hopefully there won't be any rain in the next couple of weeks, or you and Janie might not be able to open on time."

Drew prayed for the same. The weather played a big

part in meeting their deadline, but he couldn't control Mother Nature. He hadn't voiced his concern to Janie. In fact, he'd seen little of her since Riley had been released from the hospital on Tuesday. The ride home had been awkward after Drew told Janie he'd had a family but left it at that. He didn't want to go into the details of the accident and his failure to save his wife and daughter.

Janie's silence told him she'd gotten the hint. She'd never asked any more questions. She did send a text to let him know Riley was okay and anxious to help out with getting the camp ready. But Janie felt she needed to rest a few more days.

In the meantime, she'd been busy working on obtaining the proper licensing and interviewing a few architects about expanding the activity building. Drew agreed the expansion was an excellent idea. The weather wouldn't be perfect every day, so having a backup indoor facility to host games and other events was a good idea. The existing building had always been too small. Drew pulled his hammer from his tool belt and went back to work. The less time he spent thinking about Janie, the better.

In between hammering, Skip paused. "Guess who I ran into in town? Janie."

Drew flinched. *So much for keeping his mind off Janie.* "Oh yeah?"

Skip nodded. "It was the first time I've seen her since she got back into town. She looks great. Don't you think?"

Of course he did. In fact, she looked better than great. That was the problem. Janie was beautiful. She always had been. Even more of a reason to keep his mind off her and focused on the camp.

"Drew? What do you think?"

"Yeah—whatever." Drew continued hammering with hopes of giving Skip a hint to nix the Janie talk.

"What's wrong?" Skip dropped the hammer to his side. "This isn't about Lori, is it?"

Skip was a great friend, but sometimes he didn't know when to quit. Over the past several months, he'd tried to convince Drew it might be time to start dating again. He insisted it's what Lori would have wanted, but the guilt saddling him for the past two years had been overwhelming. He couldn't love another woman. Drew knew in his heart he didn't deserve a second chance at love. "I don't want to talk about Lori or Janie."

"Come on, man. I knew Lori pretty well. She wouldn't have wanted you to live the rest of your life alone. You know that, don't you? And you know she would want you to move forward with the plans you guys had made to open the outdoor center."

His mind was jumbled, and he didn't know that for sure. One thing he knew was that the less time he spent alone with Janie, the better. The sooner they could get this camp up and running, the quicker he'd be able to go back into hiding. He wasn't afraid to admit it, even if it was only to himself.

Drew had tried to hide from the world since the accident, but Mrs. Applegate's last wishes were forcing him to venture outside his comfort zone. Was the land really worth it? Taking possession of his share of the property wasn't that important to him, but it wasn't only about his share. He had to think of Janie and Riley. They needed a roof over their heads. The money from Mrs. Applegate could provide both of them with a secure future.

"No, you're right. Lori wouldn't want me to be alone,

but it's what I want." The nightmares had become more frequent and Drew knew part of the reason was obvious. Sweet little Riley. Through no fault of her own, she had turned his world upside down and brought his past back to haunt him.

"Really, man? You want to stay holed up in that cabin all alone for the rest of your life?" Skip picked up a board and placed it on the table saw. "It's bad enough you're roaming the trails by yourself all day at your job."

Drew remained silent. He wasn't going to argue with his friend. There was no way Skip could understand. As long as Drew continued to patrol his assigned territory there would be little opportunity to meet people. He'd be protecting his heart from any further pain. He didn't deserve another chance at happiness. His family had died because of his irresponsibility. He never should have gotten behind the wheel of the family's minivan. He'd worked a busy twenty-four-hour shift at the station with no sleep. Lori had pleaded with him, but in the end, he'd taken command of the wheel and in an instant, his life had changed forever. It was over.

"I don't know, Drew. I think Janie might be good for you."

Once upon a time that might have been true, but now, he wasn't good for Janie. It was better for everyone if he lived his life alone. It was the only guarantee he wouldn't fall in love again and risk heartache for a second time.

Friday morning, a glint of sun streamed through the blinds of Drew's bedroom. Outside, the daily visit from the Red-headed Woodpecker sounded against the gutter. He yanked his pillow from underneath his head to shield his eyes. Thanks to Skip's help yesterday, they'd finished the roof of the barn, but his nonstop chatter about Janie and Riley had resulted in a fitful night of sleep.

Between the sun and the bird, sleep was out of the question. Strong black coffee was in order. Drew rousted himself out of bed.

As he shuffled toward the kitchen, his phone sounded a weather alert. After turning on the coffee maker, he picked up the phone from the counter and took a seat at the kitchen table. A quick tap on the screen revealed a strong thunderstorm watch for later this afternoon. Weather-related delays—exactly what he didn't want.

Following a quick shower, Drew grabbed his keys and was headed out the door when his phone rang. Janie. The one person he wanted to keep out of his mind today, but he couldn't avoid her forever if they were going to get the camp open by the Fourth of July, so he swiped the screen to accept the call.

Ten minutes later, Drew cruised along the mountain road. With the windows of his truck open, the unusually humid air was present. Drew's mind drifted to his earlier phone conversation with Janie. She and Riley were excited for him to come out to the farm today. Janie had met with the architect yesterday and seemed anxious to share the plans on the expansion of the activity building. Riley had been resting the past few days and had begged Janie nonstop to help out today, so she'd conceded. The plan was to meet up at the barn in a half an hour. Drew was anxious to show her what he and Skip had accomplished yesterday.

He reached the end of the gravel road, parked and stepped out of his truck. He hesitated when he spotted Janie and Riley out in the field peppered with wildflowers, laughing as they chased Frankie. Observing the pair, for a second he imagined it was Lori and Heidi. Then a memory of the fiery crash snatched away the image.

"Mr. Drew!" Riley called as she ran in his direction with her arms flailing. Janie trailed behind.

Riley hugged Drew's legs, causing his chest to tighten. "I feel like I haven't seen you in forever." She looked up to him, squinting into the morning sun.

It did seem like a lifetime since he'd seen Riley's precious face. For a split second, his heart didn't hurt quite as much. He looked down and cupped his hand under her chin. "I'm glad you're feeling better, munchkin."

"Thanks to you—you saved my life." Riley paused and turned to Janie who had joined them. "That's what Mommy told me."

Drew passed a glance to Janie. She tucked a stray strand of hair behind her ear and her face flushed. "Yes, thank you again, Drew."

"You would have done the same if I hadn't been around." He was anything but a hero.

Janie stepped closer. "I'm not so sure. I've never been good in emergencies. I probably would have called nine-one-one and waited. We both know what could have happened if you hadn't made the decision to rush Riley to the hospital yourself." Janie gently placed her hand on Drew's forearm. "You saved precious minutes that could have cost my daughter her life. I'll never forget that, Drew."

As they headed toward the barn, Janie's praise caused fear and doubt to go to war inside him. He couldn't save his own family. What would she think about that? What if she found out he'd made the worst decision of his life by getting behind the wheel of the car when he'd been dog-tired? She'd think the same thing he did. He was a poor excuse for a husband, father and most of all, a protector.

Outside the barn, Janie watched Drew as he pointed toward the structure. His white-collared golf shirt accentuated his muscular shoulders. "Skip and I finished the roof yesterday."

"I can't believe it's fixed. That was a lot of work." Janie looked up and shielded the sun from her eyes.

"I told you, Mommy, Mr. Drew is like a superhero." Riley scooped Frankie into her arms.

"I can't take all of the credit. Earl and his guys had accomplished a lot before Skip and I took over," Drew added.

Janie loved how the townspeople had come together to help her reach the goal of opening by the Fourth of July. She was thankful they'd be compensated thanks to Mrs. Applegate's last wishes. The weeks were passing quickly—too quickly. "Well, thank you for taking charge and bringing your friends over to help. It really means a lot. Maybe I should have a cookout and invite everyone over." She tugged on her jacket sleeve.

"That's not necessary, but it sounds nice. We're glad to do it. Should we take a walk over to the activity building? I'm anxious to hear the architect's ideas for expansion."

"Sounds good to me," Janie responded.

Drew turned to Janie. "Maybe you should put your jacket in the car. It's going to be pretty warm today."

Janie's shoulders tensed. She couldn't let Drew see

what was under her sleeves. Even Riley had never seen her arms bare. "Oh no, I'm fine."

"Mommy doesn't like to get sun on her skin."

Janie appreciated her daughter's effort to explain. But when Drew glanced toward her shorts that exposed her legs, she knew he wasn't buying it. Winter was so much easier.

As the threesome strolled along the grassy path lined with wildflowers, the scent of honeysuckle tickled Janie's nose. "I missed that smell."

"What, Mommy?"

Janie stopped at a nearby bush, plucked a flower and trailed it underneath her nose. "This—it's honeysuckle." She guided her hand toward Riley's face.

"That smells good enough to eat." Riley grinned.

"You can. Look." Janie carefully plucked the bottom and slid the piece through the stem. "See that—it's a little dollop of honey. You can eat it."

Riley watched with her mouth open. "That's so cool. Let me try." She picked a flower off the same bush and repeated her mother's moves. "Yummy! It tastes just like the honey you put on my peanut butter sandwiches."

"Remember that summer we tried to fill an entire jar with the nectar? We thought we could start a booming business." Drew helped himself to a taste.

Janie tossed her head back and laughed. "I forgot about that. We were out here for hours. How on earth did we think we'd ever have enough to set up our own honey stand?" The memories were bittersweet. Her life now was a far cry from those carefree days of her childhood. Things had been easy. She didn't have to keep secrets.

Riley giggled. "You guys should have set up a lemonade table instead."

"You're right about that, munchkin." Drew ruffled the top of her head.

An hour later, Janie had explained the plans the architect had suggested.

"I think it's a great idea to divide the building up into different rooms. That way we can have a variety of activities going on at the same time." Drew paused. "I mean, *you* can."

"Aren't you going to help us, Mr. Drew? I thought that legal paper said you had to."

Janie watched her daughter tugging on Drew's arm. Yes, she needed his assistance to get things going, but she had to run the camp on her own. Placing her trust into another man wasn't an option. She'd made that mistake once and look where that got her. "Riley, Mr. Drew will assist us with getting the camp ready to open, but after that, we'll be running it ourselves. Remember, he has a full-time job as a park ranger."

Riley kicked up some dirt on the ground. "I don't think we can do it alone. Remember Daddy used to say you couldn't do anything unless a man told you how."

Janie's stomach soured at the mention of her ex-husband, but more so over the fact that her daughter had heard those belittling comments. Would Riley grow up thinking she couldn't do anything on her own?

Drew stepped closer to the little girl, whose eyes were glued to the ground. He placed his hand under her chin and tilted her face toward him. "Your mommy can do anything she puts her mind to. She doesn't need a man's help. And that goes for you too, remember that, okay?"

Riley nodded.

Janie yanked on each sleeve. "I think it's time we head back to the car. We've got some errands to run."

Outside the air was like a tropical rain forest. "It's so humid." Janie noticed the once-clear bluebird sky had been seized by a large wedge-shaped black cloud. Hanging low, it appeared to be moving closer. Janie had never seen something like it. Tiny hairs at the base of her neck rose.

"It feels weird out here, Mommy."

The air was still, the birds silent. Something didn't feel right. Janie pointed up toward the sky. "I've never seen a cloud like that before."

Thunder cracked.

"We have to get up to the house." Drew scooped Riley into his arms. "Get the dog, Janie. That's a shelf cloud." He grabbed Janie's hand and propelled them up the hill.

"What is that, Mr. Drew? It looks scary!"

A split second later, Janie's and Drew's phones went crazy with blaring alarms and notifications. Then an announcement sounded, "A tornado warning has been issued in your area. Take shelter immediately." Riley's question had been answered.

Chapter Six

The monstrous cloud chased the threesome. Drew's breath came in quick bursts, as he sprinted up the hill toward the house with Riley in his arms and Janie trailing behind carrying Frankie. Fat raindrops pelted his face. The winds intensified and the sky turned the color of coal. Minutes later they reached the front porch of the farmhouse, and Drew paused to catch his breath before he placed Riley on the ground.

"I'm scared, Mr. Drew!"

The nearby Leyland cypress trees swayed back and forth. Flashes of lightning lit up the sky like a beacon. Drew turned to Janie. He knew she wouldn't take possession of the house until they reopened the camp, but he held on to hope. "Do you have a key?" Tree limbs hurdled through the front yard.

"No!" Janie shouted over the rumbles of thunder.

"I'm going to have to break a window so we can get inside to the cellar." He sprinted along the side of the large wraparound porch to a stack of firewood. After snatching a log, he raced back to the front door lined with glass windowpanes on each side. "Step back!"

Janie grabbed Riley's hand and tugged her away from the door.

Drew extended his arm backward, turned his head away and with a strong push, smashed the log through the window. Shards of glass exploded in all directions. Frankie snarled. Drew placed the wood on the ground, reached inside and grabbed the door handle. With a quick turn of the lock he pushed the door open. "Hurry—we need to get inside!" He had to protect them.

Janie pulled Riley toward the entrance. The little girl whimpered.

Once inside, Drew shoved the door, but the force of the wind was stronger. Rain splashed against his face. With one more forceful push, it finally closed.

"What's that noise?" Riley called out. "It sounds like a train."

"Come on—we've got to get downstairs," Drew yelled before they tore through the hallway. He jerked open the basement door. With his other hand, he flagged them toward the steps. "Be careful!" A chill ran up his back as he yanked the door shut.

The light in the cellar was dim, but fear lit up Janie's eyes. Drew had heard a tornado could mimic the sound of a freight train approaching. He pointed to the area once used for storage. "We need to get into that room. It has cinder block walls." He remembered helping Mrs. Applegate clear out the space after her husband had passed away.

Inside the room, Riley huddled close. "I'm scared, Mr. Drew." She wrapped her arms around his waist.

Drew inhaled a steadying breath. There was no way he'd let anything happen to Riley or her mother. He scanned his surroundings. An old sofa sat on the other side. Drew raced toward it, grabbed three cushions and hurried back to the room. Janie and Riley cowered in the corner with Frankie. "Here!" He handed each a pillow. "Use this to cover your head."

For several minutes, the three hunkered down inside the windowless room trusting the cement walls would keep them safe. Drew heard the faint sounds of Riley crying and her mother trying to console her. *Please, God, help us to survive this storm, but especially protect Janie and Riley. Don't let anything happen to them.*

Moments later, the winds quieted. Only the sound of rain rushing through the gutters could be heard outside. Drew let out a sigh of relief and gave thanks to God for keeping them safe. He removed the cushion and got to his feet. "Okay, you can uncover your heads. The worst is over." But was it? Drew had no idea what waited for them once they stepped outside to access the damage. The storm had passed quickly, but he knew from watching The Weather Channel that a quick and strong tornado could do just as much damage as one moving slower.

"Do you think it's safe to go upstairs?" Janie reached for Riley's hand.

Drew scratched underneath his chin. "I'll go up first to make sure it's safe for us to walk around. Wait here. If everything is okay, I'll come back to get you."

Scaling the stairs, Drew prayed for minimal damage. Once at the top, he pushed open the door and released his breath. Nothing seemed out of place in the living room. He looked over the area. All of the windows remained intact. That was a blessing. He headed toward the front door and stepped outside on the porch. Debris littered the lawn. The oak tree that had been around as long as Drew could remember had lost a large branch, but thankfully it hadn't fallen on the house. He'd get Earl and his guys to come by with their chain saws to clear it away. When he turned to head back inside he spotted smoke billowing from the activity building. Then flames shot out from one of the windows. Drew jerked his phone from his back pocket and punched in 911.

"Nine-one-one—what's your emergency?"

He immediately recognized the voice. "Tammy, it's Drew. I'm at the Applegate farm. There's a fire in the old activity hall. I think maybe it was struck by lightning."

"Got it, Drew. I'll dispatch a truck. We've had reports of downed power lines, so it could take a while."

"Thanks, Tammy." He ended the call and pocketed his phone. Drew charged inside the house and ran down the steps into the basement. Janie and Riley remained huddled where he'd left them. "Come on—let's go!" He scooped Frankie into his arms.

"What is it, Drew?" Janie yelled while she and Riley followed behind.

"There's a fire in the activity hall. I need to get to the barn and grab a fire extinguisher. I don't know how long it will take the fire truck to get here." Drew opened the door and guided Janie and Riley outdoors.

"Wow—look!" Riley pointed toward the large tree branch on the ground.

"That could have fallen on the house." Janie's brow crinkled.

"The house looked okay. It doesn't appear to have any damage. I'll check it more closely once the fire is extinguished," Drew called out while the three ran through the meadow.

Finally at the barn, Drew went inside to grab the extinguisher mounted to the wall. Janie and Riley waited outside to catch their breath. He exited the structure. "You both stay here."

"No—I don't want you down there by yourself. You run ahead."

Drew nodded to Janie and took off down the hill. Adrenaline coursed through his veins. When he arrived at the building, he flung open the door to assess the situation. There appeared to be more smoke than flames. That was good. He pulled the pin off the extinguisher, aimed the nozzle toward the blazes and squeezed the trigger in a controlled manner. Drew swept the nozzle from side to side. Moments later, his shoulders relaxed at the sound of approaching sirens.

Within minutes, the firemen were inside the structure fighting what remained of the fire.

Drew swiped his hand across his brow and headed toward the truck where Janie and Riley safely stood, each drinking a bottle of water.

"Here, take this." Janie handed him a bottle. "They've got plenty on the truck, if you need more."

Drew accepted the offering and guzzled until it was gone. "Thank you." He ran the back side of his hand across his lips. "Are you guys okay?" He realized since the storm had approached they'd all been going full steam.

"Sure—we're fine, Mr. Drew. I can't believe you put that whole fire out by yourself. You can do anything." Riley's eyes shone bright.

That wasn't true. He couldn't do anything. What

would Riley think of him if she learned the truth? What would Janie think? His stomach rolled over.

"Drew? Are you okay?" Janie rested her hand on his forearm.

"Yeah, sure…I'm good."

The firemen exited the building and approached Drew. "It looks like everything is under control. We might need to sign you up on our team, man." Ernie Hiers patted Drew on the back. "Things could have gotten out of hand if you hadn't taken control with the fire extinguisher."

"What kind of damage are we looking at?" Drew had feared this would put him and Janie behind with the opening of the camp. As it was, they were already pressed for time.

"Actually, it's not too bad. There appears to be more smoke damage than anything. It's safe to go inside. Just give the insurance company a call and they'll recommend a restoration crew to take care of the soot. It shouldn't take more than a couple hours' work to get it cleaned up." Ernie spoke as though it was no big deal.

Drew made a note to contact Larry regarding reaching out to the insurance company. "And the roof? That's where the lightning hit that caused the fire, right?" Drew pointed.

"Exactly. It shouldn't be too big of a repair. What about the rest of the farm? Have you had a chance to look around?" Ernie checked out the property.

"We took shelter up at the house. Things seemed to be okay there. I still need to inspect the barn thoroughly." The cabins were in need of repair before the storm, so they shouldn't have many surprises there. "Thanks for coming over. I know you guys must be busy." Drew extended his hand to Ernie, nodding to the two others.

"Thank you so much, guys." Janie shook each of their hands. "We really appreciate what you do for our community."

"It's our pleasure. We're just thankful Whispering Slopes didn't get a direct hit from the tornado. With the exception of a few downed power lines, things seem to be okay." Ernie and his crew headed back to their truck.

A look of concern washed over Janie's face as she eyed the structure. "I'm afraid to see the damage."

"You heard Ernie. He said it wasn't so bad. Come on—let's go see for ourselves." Drew tossed his water bottle in the back of his truck as they headed inside the building. He hoped they would find little damage on the rest of the farm. If not, he'd be forced to spend more time with Janie and Riley. And he wasn't sure his heart could handle that.

Two hours later, after speaking with Larry Caldwell, Janie had contacted the insurance company and had been given the name of a restoration company. After a quick call, they were scheduled to take care of the cleanup tomorrow morning. Drew and Riley kept busy sweeping the floors in the activity building and picking up debris.

"Wow, you two make quite the team." Janie pocketed her cell inside her jacket. "If it weren't for the soot on the walls, you'd never know there'd been a fire." She glanced around the room.

"I'm getting hungry, Mommy," Riley called out from across the room.

Drew rubbed his stomach. "I'm a little famished myself. How about we go into town and get some lunch. One More Scoop has great burgers and they make the best chocolate milkshakes in the world."

Riley skipped across the room toward Drew. Frankie followed. "I love milkshakes, but what makes them so great?"

Drew bent down and patted the dog's head. "Well, for one thing, they're so thick you need a spoon to eat them."

Riley jumped up and down. "I love them like that!" She squealed. "What else?"

"It's got little chunks of chocolate pieces in it, too." Drew looked at Janie and winked. "Your mommy and I used to sit at the counter and share one practically every day after school."

Janie's pulse raced. Those had been some of the happiest times in her life, yet they'd been buried under years of abuse. Drew had always been so gentle and kind. He'd been exactly what she wanted in a man. How did she end up marrying someone the exact opposite? She shook away the thoughts. Her focus needed to be on the camp, not Drew.

"Mommy, can we go?"

"Come on, Janie. You'll love it. The place hasn't changed a bit. Let me give them a quick call to make sure they've got power and they're open for business."

Janie nodded. Maybe the restaurant hadn't changed, but she had. She was a far cry from that innocent young girl he'd shared milkshakes with after school.

Twenty minutes later, the bell chimed over the front door to One More Scoop. The enticing aroma of sugary waffle cones and cinnamon filled the room. Janie looked around the space. Time had stood still. A shiver traveled up her spine. If only it had.

"This place is so cool!" Riley sang out.

"Look familiar, Janie?" Drew laughed. "Where would you ladies like to sit?"

"I wanted to sit at the counter, like you and Mommy used to do." Riley bounced up and down on one foot.

Janie looked at Drew and rolled her eyes. "I really don't think this child needs any sugar."

"Aw…come on, Mommy. Let's get those seats over there." Riley pointed to the last three stools at the end of the counter.

The place was packed and chatter filled the room. As they walked through the restaurant, the temperature felt warm to Janie. Something must be wrong with the air-conditioning. Her stomach grew queasy. Situations like this, where there was no reasonable explanation for her to be wearing a jacket, were difficult. She hoped no one would mention it.

"Well hello, Drew."

Janie turned to the elderly woman who sat at a table next to the counter.

"Good afternoon, Mrs. Buser." Drew bent down to give the woman a hug.

Mrs. Buser's cheeks flushed. Drew had just made her day.

He looked around the restaurant. "It doesn't appear they sustained any damage from the storm."

"They lost power for a little while. That's why it's so hot in here. But apart from that we are all fortunate. I heard Berryville had an F1 tornado."

"Oh pardon me for being rude. You remember Janie, don't you?" Drew asked.

"Janie…I didn't know you were back in town. How are you, dear?" Mrs. Buser reached for her hand.

"I'm doing well, thank you. How are you, Mrs. Buser?"

"I'm still running Buser's General Store." She glanced at Riley. "And who is this beautiful little girl?"

Riley stepped to the edge of the table. "I'm Riley. You have your own store? How cool!"

Mrs. Buser laughed. "You'll have to come visit me sometime." She turned to Drew. "Please, join me. I hate to eat alone."

Drew looked at Janie and then to Riley. "Well, Riley had her heart set on sitting up at the counter."

Riley plopped down in the chair next to her new friend. "I'd rather sit here with Mrs. Buser." She looked around. "Besides, you can see more here."

Mrs. Buser laughed. "You sound a lot like me when I was your age, Riley. I liked to be in the center of everything."

Janie nodded. "Yep, that's Riley."

"How long are you planning to stay in Whispering Slopes, Janie?"

Janie told Mrs. Buser about inheriting the land and how she and Riley planned to stay in town permanently.

"I must be getting rusty. I usually know all of the news around here. I'm afraid I hadn't heard who had inherited sweet Mary Applegate's land. What a wonderful gift for you and Riley."

"Yeah, Mr. Drew has to help us get the camp up and running before the Fourth of July, so he can get his share of the land, too," Riley added. "And if we don't get it ready by then, everything goes to charity."

"Oh, really?" the woman commented.

Janie took notice of the wide grin igniting across Mrs. Buser's face when she spoke.

Drew exchanged a quick glance with Janie before turning back to the older woman. "You're surprised?"

"I may be wrong, but it sounds like my old friend Mary wanted to do a little matchmaking." She flashed a wink in Janie's direction.

Her stomach tightened at Mrs. Buser's remark.

A teenage girl approached the table wearing a One More Scoop T-shirt and black jeans. She pulled a pencil from her loose bun. "Hi, I'm Jenna. I'll be serving you today."

"Wow! This would be a cool place to work. Maybe I can get a job here when I'm older." Riley turned to her mother, "Can I, Mommy?"

Jenna directed her attention to Riley. "It's a lot of fun and you get all the ice cream you can eat."

"Boy, I might want to work here, too." Drew nudged Riley. "So what do you say to double cheeseburgers, fries and a chocolate-chunk milkshake?"

"Yay!" Riley cheered.

Janie rubbed her stomach. "I might need a long nap after that kind of lunch."

Drew placed the order and Jenna breezed off toward the kitchen. "No napping today. We've got a tight schedule. I thought we'd start painting the cabins."

"Do you plan to reopen those old structures, too?" Mrs. Buser took a sip of her sweet tea. "If I recall correctly, they were in need of repair."

Janie had to agree. Getting rid of the mice problem was only the beginning. From what she'd seen, the floors needed to be redone and the walls needed a fresh coat of paint, but Drew hadn't discussed it with her.

Drew intertwined his fingers and rested his hands on the table. "That's true. They are in bad shape. Since Janie doesn't plan to open for overnight guests until maybe late summer or early fall, I thought we'd remodel one cabin so we can use it as a model for the grand reopening."

He'd never mentioned that idea to her. He'd just taken charge…like her ex-husband always had.

Mrs. Buser nodded. "That's a good idea, Drew." She turned to Janie. "Honey, aren't you warm? Can I help you with your jacket?"

Janie pulled away from Mrs. Buser. "I'm fine, thanks." Sweat beaded her forehead. "I need to run to the restroom. I'll be back in a minute, Riley." She bolted out of her chair and scurried toward the women's room. Thankfully it was a single room. She slammed the door behind her and turned the lock. Trying to catch her breath, she stepped toward the sink and turned on the water. She caught her reflection in the mirror and rubbed her arms. Would she ever escape her past with this constant reminder she tried so hard to conceal?

And even though Drew told Riley differently, did he feel the same way her ex-husband did—that she wasn't capable of making any sort of decision on her own? That she could never survive without a man? Well, she could. She had to. Yes, Mrs. Applegate's last wishes had to be honored, but after that, she'd make it on her own, with Riley. No one else. Janie didn't need another man who wanted to control her.

Chapter Seven

"Are you okay, Janie?" Drew gripped the steering wheel as he backed out of the parking lot of One More Scoop. The afternoon sun bounced on his truck, creating an inferno inside. He flipped on the air-conditioning and positioned the vents. Something was up with Janie. After she had returned from the restroom she'd hardly spoken during their lunch. She'd appeared rattled when Mrs. Buser offered to take her jacket. He wasn't buying Riley's explanation about avoiding the sun. Could she have some sort of skin condition she was embarrassed for anyone to see?

Janie glanced toward the backseat where Riley sat with an earbud stuck into each ear, humming a tune. She turned her attention back to Drew and rubbed her hands on the tops of her legs. "Yes, I'm fine."

"You just seemed a little quiet while we were eating with Mrs. Buser. It wasn't what she said about Mrs. Applegate matchmaking, was it?" He half laughed in an attempt to lighten the mood. It didn't. "I hope you're not worried we won't make the deadline. I won't let that happen." He placed the truck into Drive and pressed his foot on the accelerator. "I have everything under control." Still silent, Drew observed her. There she was again, tugging on her jacket as if the sleeves weren't long enough. He put his focus back on the road. "If we're going to work together, we need to be able to communicate. I've never been a good mind reader."

"You have everything under control," she muttered.

He noticed the emphasis she put on *you*. "Excuse me?"

She squirmed in the leather seat. "I really don't want to discuss this right now." She tilted her head back toward Riley.

"She can't hear anything while she's listening to music. Come on. Tell me what's up. You used to be able to talk to me about anything." They had a lot of work ahead of them. He wanted to nip this in the bud as soon as possible.

"It's the cabins."

"What about them?"

Janie blew out a breath. "Mrs. Applegate's wishes were for us to work together to get the camp reopened." She hesitated.

"I realize that. So what's the problem?"

"You're completely taking control over everything. You didn't tell me about your plans for the cabins or that we were going to start painting today."

This was why she was upset? Didn't she understand he was doing this for her and Riley? "I'm trying to help you. I don't want you to worry that you won't have a roof over your head or money." This wasn't the Janie he remembered. She always liked when people took initiative. "Why would that bother you?"

"I only want to have an equal say in what we do

going forward." She turned her head and gazed out the window.

Clearly this conversation was over. "Point taken. I'm sorry."

Silence hung in the air during the remaining drive to the farm. Drew glanced in his rearview mirror. Riley had drifted off to sleep. "Looks like someone didn't get her rest last night."

Janie nodded. "She didn't have a good night."

The last thing Drew wanted was for Riley to be upset. Maybe he could fix the problem. "What happened?"

"Before she went to bed, we were going through some old photo albums. She started asking a lot of questions about her father." Janie shook her head. "I hate that he's made her feel this way."

"What kind of things did she want to know?"

"The same stuff she asks over and over. Why doesn't her daddy want to see her? Why didn't he want to share custody with me? It breaks my heart to see her so crushed over a man who could just walk away from his own daughter. What kind of person does that?"

Drew wasn't sure how to respond. He had always been a loving and attentive father to his daughter, Heidi. He couldn't imagine ever walking away from her intentionally, like Riley's father had. But the facts remained. God had given him this precious little girl and he failed to protect her when she needed him.

Janie sighed. "I don't want his actions to make her feel she's not wanted or loved."

"I've watched the two of you together. Trust me, Riley knows you love her. That's what's important." Drew reached for her hand. When she didn't pull it away, he took comfort in the softness of her skin. Enjoying it a little too much, he retracted his hand.

She looked down at the sudden movement. "I hope so. I'm sorry I reacted the way I did. I know you're trying to help, and I shouldn't compare you to—"

Janie didn't have to say it. She was comparing him to her ex-husband. Was he controlling in their marriage? Was that why they'd divorced? "Janie, if you ever want to talk, I'm here."

"Thank you, Drew. I appreciate the offer. I'm just not ready."

Drew nodded. Would she ever be? But how could he expect her to open up and talk about the past when he kept his dark secret locked away? It was only a matter of time before Janie learned what had happened to his family. Whispering Slopes was a small town and although the people had good intentions, they did like to talk. Wouldn't it be better for her to hear the truth from him? Maybe someday. Not today. "Why don't we swing by the paint store and get started on the cabin? You can pick out the color."

Janie stood in the center of the cabin and dipped the paintbrush into the eggshell-colored paint. She gave it a quick stir and hoped a fresh coat would clear the musty air.

"You picked a great color." Drew eyed the wall. "It really brightens up the place."

"I still think purple would be better." Riley pushed the broom across the dusty, wide-plank wood floor.

Janie and Drew laughed.

"I'm not kidding. My room in Maryland was purple. Wasn't it, Mommy?"

Drew looked to Janie for confirmation. "It's true.

When we bought the house, we told her she could have her room painted any color she wanted."

"I don't think I've ever seen a purple room. I guess it's better than black." Drew laughed and pried open another can of paint.

Riley wrinkled her nose. "Yuck! That would be too scary. The purple was really light. It was so pretty." Riley gazed toward the open front door. "It looked like that." She pointed to a nearby bush.

"Oh, lavender. That's a different story." Drew winked at Janie.

For a second, Janie's heart drummed against her ribcage. Caught off guard by the momentary attraction, she shook it away and continued to stir her paint. "Do you want me to do the trim while you do the walls?"

Drew gave her a sly grin. "Oh no. I'm not going to fall into that trap."

"What are you talking about?" Janie's brow arched.

"I pick and then I'm the control freak. You're deciding on this one." He winked.

"I never called you that." Janie looked down at the can in front of her and she couldn't resist. She plunged the brush inside, pulled it out and flicked paint in Drew's direction. Little droplets peppered his face.

Riley jumped up and down. "Paint fight! Paint fight!"

"Oh no, you didn't!" Drew returned fire, splattering Janie's face.

Janie looked at Riley who laughed before she threw her hand over her mouth. "Sorry, Mommy, but it was funny."

Drew and Janie nodded at each other. They dunked their brushes and ran toward Riley catching her off guard. With a glob of paint on each cheek, Riley's laughter filled the room.

"This is the most fun ever!" the child squealed.

Janie's heart soared. She loved to see her little girl so happy. She'd had such a difficult time during the divorce. Still, Janie couldn't help but worry about the attachment Riley had to Drew. The last thing she wanted was for her daughter to endure more pain. If Riley imagined a happy family scenario in her head, it would only lead to heartache. A relationship with Drew wasn't possible.

"Okay, ladies, we've got too much work to do to horse around."

"Yeah, Mommy. You started it."

Janie shot a glance at Drew. "You made me do it."

He laughed, grabbed a smaller brush off the counter and handed it to Janie. "Alright, I'll accept blame. If it's okay with you, you can use this to knock out the trim work. Since your hands are smaller, you can reach the corners easier. Riley and I will work on the larger areas. I'll use the roller brush."

Janie nodded in agreement.

"What am I going to use, Mr. Drew?"

Drew bent down. "You, young lady, will have the most important job."

A huge smile spread across her daughter's face. "Really? What will I do?"

"Actually, two things. First, you'll carry the bucket for me as we work our way around the cabin. I've poured half of the paint into an empty can so it's not too heavy for you."

"What else? What else?" Riley chirped.

"You'll tell me if I missed a spot. But your eyes have to be really good for that job." He glanced at Janie. "How are they?"

Riley's eyes opened like giant saucers. "They're really good. Look—" she pointed "—I can see farther away than most people."

Drew chuckled. "Is that so? Okay then, let's all get to work."

Two hours later Janie's knees ached despite the throw pillow Drew had given her earlier. "I think we might need to wrap it up for today."

"Ahh, Mommy, I don't want to go home yet."

Janie eyed Riley. She stuck to Drew's side like a burnt chocolate-chip cookie on an ungreased baking sheet. "We need to go grocery shopping before we head home. I want to pick up some garlic bread to go with the spaghetti."

"Can Mr. Drew come over for dinner? Please, Mommy!"

Janie glanced over toward Drew who was finishing up the wall closest to the front door. Had he heard Riley's request?

"Can he?" Riley asked even louder.

Janie bit the side of her mouth. He definitely heard that. Maybe she should invite him. After all, he was using his vacation time to help her meet the deadline. Yes, he'd get some land, but she had so much more at stake. She swallowed the lump that clogged her throat and sauntered toward him. "Drew, would you like to come over for dinner tonight? I'm making spaghetti."

Riley tore across the room, holding her breath until she heard his answer.

"That's my favorite," he answered.

"Mine too! Will you come?" Riley begged.

"If you let me bring the dessert." He ruffled Riley's hair.

She grinned. "That's a deal. Will you bring German chocolate cake?"

"Riley, Mr. Drew can bring whatever is most convenient for him. You shouldn't be making any special orders."

"Sorry." Riley rolled her eyes to the floor.

"Hey, munchkin." Drew reached and lifted her chin. "What makes that cake so special?"

"My daddy always bought one for me on my birthday." She shot a look at Janie. "It was his favorite, too."

"I've always been a big fan of German chocolate." Drew rubbed his stomach.

Janie had a recipe for the cake. It had been in her family for generations. Shortly after she'd married Riley's dad, she surprised him by baking the cake for his birthday. He'd told her it was the worst he'd ever eaten. She never baked it again. Shaking off the memory, she headed to the counter and grabbed her purse. She reached inside, snatched her car keys and glanced at her watch. "Does seven o'clock work for you?"

"Sounds great. I'll finish cleaning up and run home for a quick shower." Drew followed the two and opened the door to the cabin. "Be safe driving."

Thoughts swirled through Janie's head as she and Riley walked to the car. Did she really just invite Drew to dinner? Was she sending Riley the wrong message? That there was more to her relationship with Drew than an old friend helping her. She hoped not because that was all that was going on here. Wasn't it?

An hour later, Janie stood at the kitchen sink. She swiped the romaine lettuce under the cold water rushing from the brushed-nickel spigot. With the oven preheating for garlic bread and the zesty meat sauce bubbling on the stove top, the room smelled like an Italian bistro. Italy—one of the many places her ex promised to take her before they were married.

"That smells yummy, Mommy," Riley called out from the family room. She and Frankie sat parked in front of the television watching a movie.

Janie always loved to cook despite her ex-husband's constant criticism of every meal she made. The dicing and slicing had been a way to escape her abusive marriage. Now free from the past, she still found solace in preparing food for herself and Riley. She blotted the lettuce with a paper towel. Was she truly free? The visible and emotional scars were a constant reminder. Could she ever trust her judgment when it came to men?

The doorbell chimed and pulled Janie from her thoughts.

"He's here. He's here!" Riley called out. She raced to the door with Frankie trailing behind, his toenails scratching against the hardwood floor.

Janie picked up her phone to take a quick peek at herself with her camera. Why was she so nervous? Sure, he was gorgeous, but she'd known Drew all of her life. He was just a friend helping her. She placed the device back on the counter, straightened her shoulders and headed to the family room.

"Look, Mommy! Mr. Drew brought a German chocolate cake." Riley pointed to the red-and-white box containing the dessert.

Drew stepped inside, dressed in relaxed jeans and a red polo shirt. "Wow, it smells like a gourmet Italian restaurant."

"Mommy's a really good cook. Her spaghetti and meatballs are the best!"

"Thank you, sweetie." Janie released a contented sigh and looked up at Drew. "It was nice of you to bring Riley's favorite. Can I get you something to drink? Soda, water or sweet tea?"

"Tea sounds perfect." Drew followed Janie into the kitchen.

Janie retrieved three glasses from the cherry cabinet and filled each one with crushed iced from the refrigerator. She placed the glasses on the granite counter and turned to retrieve the tea. Slowly she poured the beverage and passed one to Drew.

"What's in your briefcase, Mr. Drew?" Riley pointed to the leather satchel.

"Riley, don't be so nosy," Janie reprimanded.

Drew stowed the bag on the built-in desk underneath the cabinets. "It's okay, Riley. After we eat, I thought I'd run a couple of ideas I had by you and your mommy."

Janie reduced the heat underneath the pot of boiling noodles. "Looks like these might be ready."

"Can I help?" Drew moved closer and his arm brushed against hers, igniting a shiver. Ten years of marriage and her ex-husband had never offered his assistance.

"Yes, thank you. If you could take the noodles off the stove, I'll grab the colander."

Seconds later Drew stepped closer with the pot in hand. His spicy scent reminded her of a crisp autumn day at an outdoor festival. He carefully emptied the pot while Janie held the colander to drain the noodles over the sink.

He turned to her and she could feel his breath. "We make a pretty good team, don't we?"

Janie was no longer nervous. Panic mode had taken over. Drew's proximity was unnerving. Her reaction to him had caught her off guard. *Don't drop the noodles*.

"Mommy, isn't Mr. Drew nice? Daddy never helped you in the kitchen."

Janie flinched at her daughter's comment. She couldn't be angry at Riley. She'd spoken the truth.

"Well, I love to be in the kitchen. I only wish I was a better cook." Drew placed the pot on the counter.

"Mommy loves to cook. Maybe she can teach you!"

Janie's invitation to Drew had filled Riley's head with all sorts of crazy ideas. "Riley, why don't you take Frankie outside. He needs to get a little exercise. Dinner will be ready in a couple of minutes."

"Okay. Come on, Frankie." Riley picked up her dog and the two breezed out the back door.

"I'm sorry. Riley has a tendency to say whatever pops into her head."

Drew laughed. "There's no need to apologize. There's nothing sweeter than a child who speaks from the heart."

Janie considered his words. "What Riley said about her father was true." Should she be opening the door to a conversation she wasn't sure she was prepared to have?

"The kitchen wasn't his thing?" Drew's left brow arched.

"Pretty much. But then again, being a husband and a father wasn't his thing either."

Drew nodded. "I guess some men aren't meant to be married."

"Are you including yourself?" Janie recalled his

statement about having a family. She couldn't imagine Drew would walk out on his responsibilities, but then again, she never thought her ex would turn out to be such a cruel man.

"What do you mean?"

Janie grabbed the pot holder off the counter to remove the toasted garlic bread from the oven. "Before, you said you had a family—past tense."

Drew took a sip of his tea. "I did. I had a wife and a little girl. They were killed two years ago in a car accident."

Janie's stomach turned over. "Oh Drew, I had no idea. I'm so sorry." She placed her hand on his arm and the two stood in silence.

The back door flew open and Riley came skipping through the kitchen with Frankie on her heels. "Is dinner ready? I'm starving, Mommy."

Janie's and Drew's eyes connected before he turned to pick up the drinks and carried them to the table.

What a tragic loss he'd experienced. She couldn't imagine what he'd been through the past couple of years. She watched Drew as he and Riley played with the dog. Did her daughter's presence fill a void or was she a constant reminder of what he had lost? Janie prayed it wasn't the latter.

Chapter Eight

Drew took the final swig of his second cup of strong black coffee, preparing to meet with Janie and the architect to go over the renovation plans for the activity building. He'd decided whatever Janie wanted, he'd agree to it. The camp would belong to her after the Fourth, so she should be the one to make the final decisions. It had become obvious to him from the exchange she and Riley had at Huggamug with Molly that Janie's ex-husband probably had some control issues. Drew didn't want to be like him.

His eyes fixed on the *Whispering Slopes Times* he'd tossed on the kitchen table earlier. He picked it up and glanced at the front page. The traveling petting zoo and carnival would be in town a week from today. He rested the paper back on the table. Riley would love that.

Drew snatched his phone from his pocket before he had time to second-guess his decision. He scrolled through his contacts. Janie. Squaring his shoulders, he pressed the call button and exhaled.

"Hi, Drew. What's up?" Her voice sounded sweet as

the peonies that filled the valley. "You're still coming to meet with the architect this morning, aren't you?"

Drew grinned. Even though Janie had stressed she wanted to do everything herself, she needed his help. He liked the idea of the two of them working as a team for a common goal. Had Mrs. Applegate hoped that by carrying out her last wishes, he and Janie would be reunited as something more than friends? Was Mrs. Buser right? Had Mrs. Applegate intended to play matchmaker while securing Janie's and Riley's futures?

As much as Drew hated to disappoint his dear friend, there was no way he could allow anything to develop between him and Janie. "I'm not bailing on you. I plan to be there at eleven sharp. I was calling about something else. I didn't want to bring it up in front of Riley in case you didn't think it was a good idea. It has to do with some of the plans I wanted to discuss with you last night, but we never had a chance."

"Sure, what is it?" Janie sounded curious.

Drew studied the news article. "Next Saturday, the Black River Annual Petting Zoo and Carnival will be in Whispering Slopes. I thought it would be something Riley would enjoy. Would the two of you like to join me? It's a huge attraction for this area. It always brings in a big crowd."

A moment of silence hung in the air as Drew waited for her response. Did she think he was asking her out? "It's not a date, Janie," he added.

"I know. It's for Riley. I think she would really enjoy it. Thank you for thinking of us…I mean, her."

"Great, so it's a date." Wait, didn't he just say it wasn't? "Sorry, I—"

Janie laughed. "I know what you meant, Drew. Don't worry about it."

His shoulders relaxed. "Thanks. I'll pick you around ten a.m. next Saturday."

"I'll put it on my calendar."

Drew reached for a pen and stood from the table. He walked to the calendar hanging on his refrigerator, circled Saturday, June 20 and smiled. "I got it on mine. I'll see you at the farm in a little while."

He disconnected the call and placed his phone on the table. As much as he tried to tell himself it was best to keep his relationship with Janie and Riley all business, he couldn't help but be excited about a day spent with them that didn't include working toward opening on the Fourth of July. Whether this was right or wrong, he was following his heart for the first time since it was shattered two years ago.

When Drew arrived at the farm, he pulled his truck up in front of the activity building. Outside he spotted Janie speaking with the architect she'd hired. Jeremy Waters held an iPad and appeared to be showing her some photos as she pointed at the device, nodding her head. She was dressed in pink capris with her hair pulled back in a ponytail, but the white sweatshirt she wore captured his attention. The temperature was already in the middle eighties.

He released the seat belt, swung his legs out of the truck and headed toward Janie. The sky was a brilliant blue with billowy white clouds dotting God's canvas. Drew inhaled the clean mountain air. There was no place else he'd ever want to live.

"Hey, Drew. You know Jeremy."

Drew nodded. "Sure. It's been a while. How are you doing, man?" Jeremy had grown up in Whispering Slopes. He had around twenty years on Drew, but he was in great shape. With a hint of gray around his temples, he looked younger than his age.

Jeremy extended his hand. "I can't complain. Business is good, so that's always a blessing."

Drew turned toward Janie. "Where's the munchkin?"

"She's down at the barn playing farmer with her pretend goats. She said she needed to hand-feed the baby goats with a bottle today." Janie pushed a strand of hair caught up in the breeze away from her face. "She's got quite the imagination when it comes to animals. If she had her way, she'd want us to own an entire barn full of critters."

Drew liked the sound of this. He'd been contemplating the idea and thought it might be a good attraction for the camp. Learning how to care for them could be a great experience for the children, especially for kids who came from the city. "Well, she might be onto something."

Janie's brow arched. "What do you mean?"

"That's part of the reason I invited you both to the carnival next Saturday." Drew slid his hands into the pockets of his jeans.

"I remember as a child getting so excited to see all of the animals. I begged my dad to buy me a baby goat and a pig," Jeremy recalled.

"So you want Riley to hound me even more about filling our farm with livestock?" Janie questioned Drew.

"Well, not exactly. I think having a few animals might be a big draw for the camp."

"Drew's right, Janie. Not many kids can resist a pony or a baby goat," Jeremy added.

Janie eyed both men. "I don't know. It sounds like a lot of extra work. I'll have enough to handle without caring for animals, too."

"I can help." Drew surprised himself blurting out the offer. His heart had spoken before his head. Could he make a commitment to help Janie with the animals? When he thought of Riley, his heart warmed. Of course he could do it for her.

"Do you mind if I think about it? Right now I feel like I've got so much on my plate."

Drew nodded. "Sure. Why don't we head inside and let Jeremy show us his ideas for the renovations?"

As the threesome entered the building, Drew let excitement bubble up inside him. He hoped once Janie cuddled with those baby animals at the fair she'd have a change of heart. Without a child of his own to love and nurture, maybe bringing some joy into Riley's life could be good for all of them.

Saturday morning, Janie changed her outfit three times. The weatherman reported another hot day ahead. She stood in front of the mirror looking at her arms and a shiver rattled through her body. *You're worthless. I should have never married you. You can't do anything.* His words played through her mind. Even after a year of therapy, there were times she questioned whether her ex-husband had been right. No. She wouldn't let him ruin her day with Drew and Riley. She couldn't give him that kind of control over her. Never. And she wouldn't allow another man to have that much power over her, either.

"Mommy, are you ready yet?" Riley's sweet voice echoed in the hall before she and Frankie wandered into the bedroom. "Can you please tell me where we are going today? Why does it have to be a secret?"

Janie quickly buttoned the red long-sleeved blouse as her daughter approached. One day, she'd explain to Riley about her arms, but for now, she was too young to learn the truth.

"You look pretty, Mommy." Riley hopped up on the bed. "I hope I'm as pretty as you when I get older."

"Aw…thank you, sweetie. You're beautiful now." She strolled to her child and kissed the top of her head. "How is it that you know just the right thing to say at the perfect time?"

Riley shrugged her shoulders. "Maybe I'm like that lady on the commercial who says she can read people's minds." She giggled.

"Maybe so." Janie grabbed a pair of white leather sandals and slid each one on to her feet. They'd be doing a lot of walking today, so she wanted to be comfortable.

"I think I can read Mr. Drew's mind."

Janie turned to Riley. "Oh, you can now?"

"Uh-huh. I think he really likes you, but for some reason he's afraid to tell you."

Janie's stomach fluttered at her daughter's observation. "What makes you think that, sweetie?"

"I just see the way he looks at you. He thinks you're really pretty." She paused and looked up at Janie. "Maybe since my real daddy doesn't want me, Mr. Drew would."

Again, anger toward her ex filled her. It was one thing to make his wife feel worthless, but it was something else when he did it to his own daughter. Janie was like a protective mamma bear. She wasn't going to let her ex, or any man, ever let her daughter question her worth. "Come on, sweetie. Let's go feed Frankie. Mr. Drew will be here any minute."

Fifteen minutes later, Drew arrived and the three were on their way to the carnival.

"Can you please tell me now?" Riley called out from the backseat. Drew had asked Janie not to tell Riley where they were going so he could surprise her.

Janie turned to Drew. "This has been my world all morning."

Drew removed one hand from the wheel and covered his mouth. "Sorry." He replaced his grip.

Janie stole quick glances at Drew's chiseled profile. His freshly showered scent tickled her nose.

"Don't you like surprises, munchkin?" Drew said to Riley.

Janie turned around to see Riley with her arms crossed over her chest and her lip rolled. "Not when it's kept a secret forever."

The grown-ups shared a laugh.

"It looks like it's going to be a beautiful day." Drew pulled the visor down to block the sunlight.

Janie nodded and glanced out the car window at the mountainous landscape. "I can't believe our grand opening is coming up so fast." She rubbed her palms over her thighs. "I'm starting to get a little nervous that we're not going to get everything done."

"Try not to worry. If we focus on what has to be finished in order to open, like the repairs and getting the activity building ready so we can serve meals, everything else will come in time."

He reached over, took her hand and gave it a squeeze.

Janie flinched at his touch and Drew quickly placed his hand back on the wheel. She ran her fingers through her cascading loose curls that she'd spent twenty minutes creating, earlier. "I know you're right. Worrying isn't going to accomplish anything. At least Jeremy was able to get a large crew. They should have the kitchen up and running by later today."

"What time did they plan to start this morning?" Drew asked, flipping on the turn signal.

"Jeremy told me they'd be at the farm around seven o'clock."

"I have all of the confidence in the world with Jeremy. He knows our timeline is tight. He'll make sure the work is done. Try not to worry, Janie."

Squeals of delight ignited from the backseat when Drew turned at the sign reading Black River Annual Petting Zoo and Carnival.

"Is that the surprise, Mr. Drew?" Riley bounced up and down pointing out the window.

"It sure is, munchkin," Drew sang out as he navigated the grassy parking lot. "Are you ready to have some big fun today?"

"Oh yes! I can't wait to see the baby goats!"

Janie glanced at Drew and rolled her eyes.

"You'll be seeing a lot of different animals." Drew placed the truck into Park and jumped out of the vehicle. He rounded the front and opened Janie's door.

Janie's pulse quickened when Drew took her hand to help her out of the car. She couldn't remember the last time a man had performed such a simple gesture. "Thank you." Her cheeks warmed.

Drew opened the back door and unfastened the belt. Riley bounded from her booster seat that Janie had placed in the car earlier. "Where are we going first? Oh wow, look at that Ferris wheel! It's huge!"

Drew laughed. "Pace yourself, munchkin. We've got a lot of things to see and do."

Janie looked over the opened field now transformed into a child's dream come true. The scent of sweet waffle cones and popcorn filled the air. Laughter and music could be heard along with the occasional ringing of bells and whistles from the various games. In the distance, roosters crowed and horses neighed. "Riley, stay close. It's crowded. We don't want to get separated."

"Okay, Mommy."

Janie looked at Drew. "What's first on the list?"

Drew kneeled in front of Riley. "Today is your day. You decide what we do." He stood, removed the sunglasses from the top of his head and slid them on.

"Cool! I've never had my own day before. Let's see." Riley strummed her fingers along her chin. "The line for the Ferris wheel doesn't look too long. Let's go there first."

Drew bowed. "Okay, the Ferris wheel it is."

Riley cheered as the three headed toward the ride. For a second, Janie felt like they were a family.

As they got closer to the Ferris wheel, Janie realized it was so much bigger than it had looked in the distance. She leaned toward Drew. "Do you think Riley is big enough to go on this?"

"Sure, Mommy." Riley pointed. "The sign says five and up. I'm seven and I'm definitely tall enough."

Janie squinted up at the sun. "I don't know about this. It seems so high," she whispered.

"I can hear you, Mommy. I'm not afraid, plus the rules say I can go," Riley pleaded. "Mr. Drew said it was my day."

Drew stepped in the direction of the elderly man in charge of monitoring the line to make sure the children reached the height requirement. "Excuse me, sir."

"Yes. How can I help you?"

"Can the three of us ride together?" Drew pointed at Janie, then Riley.

The worker glanced down at Riley and smiled. "Of course. The seat is wide enough to hold two adults and a child."

"Problem solved. Riley can sit in between us. She'll be perfectly safe, Janie. Don't worry."

Riley grinned at Drew. "See, Mommy."

Janie shrugged her shoulders. "I guess I'm outnumbered."

As the party of three snaked through the line, Riley chatted with another little girl who expressed her fear about the ride. Janie listened with pride while her daughter reassured the child there was nothing to be afraid of and if she was riding with her father, she'd be perfectly safe.

"We're next! We're next!" Riley shouted when the empty car came to a stop.

Janie climbed aboard first, then helped Riley, who was covered in smiles.

Finally, Drew took a seat. Riley nuzzled between the two adults.

"This is going to be so much fun!" Riley announced.

When the car inched forward the little girl squealed with excitement. Seconds later, the ride came to a halt. "Hey, why did we stop already?"

"They have to load everyone," Drew explained.

A couple of minutes later they were at the top. Janie looked down and found herself feeling a little queasy.

"It's been a long time since I've been on this ride." Her stomach rolled. She shouldn't have eaten breakfast so late. "I forgot how much I don't like heights."

Drew shot a look of concern. "Are you okay? Do you think you're going to be sick?"

"Oh no! Please don't lose your cookies on me, Mommy. These are my brand-new shorts." Riley motioned to the neon pink clothing.

Despite the nausea, Janie chuckled. "I'm okay. My stomach is just a little unsettled. I shouldn't have been looking down." She closed her eyes. "That's better."

With everyone loaded, the music streamed from a nearby intercom, and the ride went into full swing gliding through the warm breeze.

Janie watched Riley. She couldn't remember the last time she'd seen her daughter so happy. Moving to Whispering Slopes had been good for her—good for both of them. Soon they'd have a home and, hopefully, a profitable business. Something her ex-husband said she could never do on her own.

"Isn't this the best day ever, Mr. Drew?"

"I think you're right, munchkin."

"And you know what else is good?"

"What?" Drew asked.

"It just started." Riley spread her arms open.

Drew winked at Janie. "Yes it has, Riley."

Janie caught a glimpse of Riley reaching for Drew's hand and her heart lightened. She loved to see Riley happy, but Drew might not always be around. Where would that leave her daughter? With a shattered heart—again.

As she surveyed the crowd below, Janie's eyes popped. She looked closer and her heart raced. Was that Riley's father? It couldn't be. She watched as he worked his way through the crowd. Was he looking for them? Why else would he be here?

"Hey." Drew reached over and placed his hand on Janie's tense arm. "Is your stomach feeling better?"

She pulled her eyes away from the crowd below. "Yes. Thank you." Were her eyes playing tricks? When she looked down again, the man was gone. She wrapped her arms around her waist. Her stomach wasn't better…not in the least. Was it him? She couldn't be sure.

Chapter Nine

"Do you guys want go on another ride or should we check out the petting zoo?" Drew inquired once the threesome had their feet back on the trampled fescue grass.

"Let's go see the animals!" Riley jumped up and down flapping her arms.

Drew waited for Janie's input. She'd been quiet since midway through their ride on the Ferris wheel. She kept turning around like she was looking for someone.

"Janie? Do you have a preference?"

"I'm sorry. What did you say?"

"I asked what you ladies wanted to do next," Drew repeated. Something was up with her. She seemed so distracted all of a sudden. Maybe the crowds were bothering her. Drew had never seen this many people at the carnival, and he was feeling a little uncomfortable himself.

"Oh, sorry. Whatever Riley would like to do is fine." She glanced over her shoulder.

"Okay, animals it is." Drew announced as Riley grabbed his hand and he looked down.

She grinned. "It's pretty crowded in here. You don't want to lose me."

This little girl was tugging on his heartstrings. Emotions that he'd tried to keep buried resurfaced.

The aroma of fresh hay and manure lingered in the warm air as they reached the corral housing the pygmy goats. Riley squealed with delight. "Look, you can go inside and play with them!" She pulled her hand from his.

"Well, it is a petting zoo." Drew laughed.

"Can I go inside, Mommy?"

"Yes, but stay where I can keep an eye on you."

Riley raced toward the gate, kicking up dirt under her feet. She let herself inside the pen and a caramel-colored goat with black markings bounded toward her.

Drew turned to Janie. "It looks like she made a new friend."

When she didn't respond, Drew stepped closer. "Is something wrong? You've been quiet since the Ferris wheel."

She pulled on her sleeve. "No—it's…never mind. It's silly. I thought I recognized someone, but it probably wasn't. So are these the kind of goats you think I should have for the camp?"

With the sudden change of subject, Drew assumed Janie didn't want to discuss who she thought she may have seen, so he let it go. "Yeah, they're called pygmy goats. They're pretty cool, don't you think?"

Janie's gaze drifted over the animals, and she smiled at Riley rolling on the ground with her new friend. "Yes, they are adorable, but I'm sure they're a lot of work."

"Not really."

She laughed. "Yeah, I suppose one little goat couldn't be too much trouble."

Drew bit down on his lower lip. "Two."

"What?" Janie's face crinkled.

"Well, you can't just buy one goat. They need a companion."

"I see." Janie put her hands on her hips. "It seems you've done some research. What else do they need?"

"Most important, a secure shelter to keep the predators out. But you have the barn, so that's not an issue. A couple changes would be necessary with the individual stalls, but nothing major. They also like to have access to an open area to graze, which you also have."

A smile parted her lips. "Yes, I do. What else?"

"During the winter months, you can feed them hay."

"Who can?"

"I will." Drew corrected himself before she squashed his idea. He watched Riley who was still enthralled with the goat. "If having goats makes her smile like that, I'll do whatever I can to help."

"I hate to say it because the last thing we need is something else on our plate, but you're right. She is in love with that little fella." A tear rolled down her cheek.

"What is it?"

Janie pulled a tissue from the pocket of her jeans, then dabbed her eyes. "I just can't help but wonder about the long-term effects her father's behavior will have on her. Will she grow up not trusting men?"

Drew looked at her for a long moment. "She doesn't seem to feel that way about me."

"You're right," she confessed in a trembling whisper. "She thinks you're some sort of superhero. You're so good with her." Her gaze dropped to the ground. "I really do appreciate the time and attention you give to her. I know it means a lot to her—it means so much to me, too."

Had God brought Janie and Riley back into his life for some purpose? He'd been reluctant to talk about his family in any detail, but was that really a good thing? Keeping everything bottled up inside couldn't be healthy. A part of him was afraid to open up about the past. Would Janie think less of him if she found out he wasn't man enough to save his own family?

"Drew? Where did you just go?"

He leaned against the split rail fence and swallowed hard to force the lump down his throat. "My daughter's name was Heidi. She would have been Riley's age—if I'd saved her."

Janie's face went blank. She slowly cupped her hand over her mouth, standing silent for a moment.

Children's laughter filled the air, a contrast to the regret swarming in his mind like bees. This was a mistake. He should have waited until after the camp was reopened.

"I'm so sorry, Drew. I…I don't know what to say."

Drew was familiar with people not knowing how to respond. What to say. What not to say. "My family and I were on our way to see my in-laws in North Carolina. I was working as a paramedic. I had just come off a twenty-four-hour shift. My wife didn't think it was a good idea for me to drive, but I drank a couple cups of coffee and told her I would be fine." He blew out a strong breath and closed his eyes. "Turns out, I wasn't fine. I fell asleep behind the wheel. Our van went off the road and down an embankment. The impact caused the electrical system to malfunction, igniting a fire. I couldn't—"

"Drew, stop. You don't need to say any more." Janie moved closer and took him in her arms. "I'm so sorry."

He pulled back, mashing his palms into his eyes before he could look at Janie again. "I don't want your pity. I made the mistake of getting behind the wheel." He sucked in a breath. "It's something I'll have to live with forever. I should have saved them."

The scene was ingrained in his mind. After the car rolled four times, things got fuzzy. He remembered calling out to his family, but the air had been still. Then he spotted the flames and he panicked. A trained paramedic and he froze.

"Please, don't blame yourself, Drew." She rested her hand on his forearm.

Drew looked over at Riley on the ground, surrounded by three pouncing goats, "I thought I was dealing with it pretty well. At least the nightmares had stopped, up until—"

Janie's hand dropped. "Until we moved to Whispering Slopes and you were forced to spend time with Riley. Oh, Drew, I wish you would have said something earlier. I could have kept her away, prevented her from becoming so attached to you."

He pulled in a long, slow breath to center himself. "At first, when the dreams started again, I wanted her to stay away. I didn't want to be anywhere close to that sweet little girl who was a constant reminder of not only what I'd lost, but my failure as a man. But lately, my dreams have changed. I'm not afraid to go to sleep at night," Drew confessed.

"I'm happy to hear that, Drew. But please, if it's too difficult to be around Riley, I can make arrangements for her when we have to work together. Mrs. Buser has already volunteered to babysit anytime I need her. Or we can just split up the list of projects and take care of our portions separately."

Drew considered Janie's suggestion. It would be easier to work independently in order to avoid Riley. Was that what he wanted? Not if he was being truthful to himself. Was God using Janie and Riley to nudge him out of hiding? Did He want Drew to stop living like a hermit in his cabin and on the trails? Could he do that? Drew shook his head. "According to Mrs. Applegate's wishes, we have to work together until the camp is opened." And then what? He would go back into seclusion? When he looked at Janie and her daughter he realized what he wanted, but he knew in his heart he didn't deserve it.

Janie's alarm clock buzzed, interrupting a dream about her ex-husband. No doubt, it had been prompted by seeing his lookalike at the carnival. There was no way he'd come to Whispering Slopes, especially since she'd heard from a friend in Maryland about his new girlfriend. But that was old news to Janie.

She reached toward the nightstand and mashed her hand on the off button. As she rolled onto her side, a glimmer of the early Tuesday sun peeked through the lace curtains. Her sister-in-law Joy had done a beautiful job decorating their home. The guest room was filled with antique white furniture. A club chair with seafoam-green upholstery sat next to the window, offering an invitation of an afternoon savoring a good book. The room reminded Janie of a cozy beach house.

She rested her head back onto the fluffy down pillow and her thoughts turned to Drew and the family he'd lost. It had been difficult for him to tell her about the accident, but she was happy he had. Even though he'd reminded her about the terms of the will and having to work together, since the carnival they hadn't seen each other. He'd been working with the crew on remodeling the barn and the activity building, while she'd been interviewing a few candidates for camp counselor positions and dealing with licensing issues. A little space between them was probably a good thing, but more important, Janie thought it best if Riley kept her distance from Drew. He didn't need a constant reminder of his little girl, and she didn't want Riley to get more attached than she already was.

Twenty minutes later, following a quick shower, Janie's sock-covered feet glided toward her brother's kitchen for a cup of coffee. Frankie scratched at the door waiting to go outside. "Just a minute, buddy. Let me get my caffeine fix and we'll head outside." Frankie whimpered in response and plopped down on the hardwood.

With the piping brew in her hand, Janie and the dog stepped out onto the porch that stretched across the entire front of her brother's house. This was her favorite part of the structure. Two massive columns on each side of the steps gave the home a Southern feel. Janie settled in to one of the four graceful wooden rockers perfectly aligned to focus on the stunning view of the mountains.

Moments later the screen door squeaked open. "Good morning, Mommy."

Riley stepped outside dressed in her polka-dotted nightgown, her hair a tousled mess. "Hey, sweetie." She opened up her arms and her daughter climbed onto her lap, resting her head against Janie's chest. "Did you sleep well?"

"Uh-huh."

Janie was well aware that mornings like this wouldn't last forever. Riley would grow and no longer sit with her, but for now, she'd cherish every second. She stroked her child's soft, downy hair. "Are you excited to spend the day with Mrs. Buser?"

Riley perked up and turned to her mother. "Yes! She said I could work the cash register."

On Sunday evening Drew had called to invite her and Riley on a hike today. He thought it would be good for her to familiarize herself with some of the trails before guests started to arrive. It sounded like a smart idea, but she'd suggested Riley stay with Mrs. Buser. "That sounds like fun. You always loved your toy cash register." Janie recalled how her daughter's eyes would light up whenever the drawer opened and the bell rang.

"Yeah. She also told me I could help her with the inventory. And after we're finished, she'd make ice-cream sundaes."

"You're going to have a fun day."

Her daughter turned so their noses were almost touching. "Are you excited about your date with Mr. Drew?" Riley giggled.

"It's not a date, Riley. It's for business," Janie explained.

"Going on a hike alone together sounds like a date to me." Sounding like an adult, Riley climbed off her mother's lap and sat in the rocker next to her.

When Drew first invited her on the hike, Janie had to admit, she thought he was asking her out, too. Or had it been wishful thinking? In the end, once he explained the reason behind the invitation, she realized keeping their relationship on a business level made much more sense. She would never want to run the risk of ruining their friendship or put herself in a position where she had to tell him about the abuse that went on during her marriage. Drew might be ready to share his past, but Janie would take hers to the grave. "Well, it's not a date, so let's change the subject and get some breakfast."

Riley jumped to her feet. "Let's make pancakes. I'm starving."

Janie glanced at her watch. She'd told Mrs. Buser she'd drop off Riley at ten o'clock before meeting up with Drew at the farm. "We only have an hour before you need to be at the store. How about we go into town for bagels and cream cheese?"

Riley skipped toward the door. "That sounds yummy! Can I get the strawberry cream cheese? That's my favorite."

"Mine, too. Let's go get you dressed." Janie trailed behind her daughter, excited about the day ahead.

Shortly after ten, Janie had dropped off Riley at Mrs. Buser's store and was headed to meet Drew. This would be the first time since they were kids that they'd be spending an extended period of time alone. She tried to convince herself that she wasn't excited, but her fluttering pulse told her otherwise.

Grateful for the scattered cloud cover today, she rolled down the car window, inhaling the invigorating mountain air. The slightly cooler temperature was a blessing, especially today. Wearing a jacket while hiking in June could get a little uncomfortable, not to mention spark some questions.

At the farm, she spotted Drew's truck. She couldn't wait to tell him that Riley had talked her into purchasing the pygmy goats. When she'd gone inside the corral on Saturday and played with the adorable balls of fur, she'd been a goner. Now she entertained the idea of buying a couple horses. Of course, she hadn't mentioned it to Riley in case she decided against it. She wanted to get Drew's thoughts on the issue.

As she put her car into Park and removed the key from the ignition, Drew came out of the barn. Her heart quickened exactly how it did when they were younger. He'd always been handsome. Janie recalled how every girl in school wanted to be his girlfriend, but he never really dated. Now, as a grown man, he was just plain gorgeous. Tall and lean with a perfect build, he didn't seem to realize how many heads he turned everywhere he went. That made him even more attractive.

"Well, hello there." Drew sauntered toward the car and removed his sunglasses. His eyes twinkled, causing her insides to tingle.

Janie stepped out of the vehicle. *It's not a date. It's not a date.* She needed to keep reminding herself of this.

"I have a surprise for you." He reached for her hand and guided her toward the barn.

"You know I've never been one for surprises."

Drew laughed. "I remember, but trust me. You're going to love this one."

Janie's eyes popped when she stepped inside the barn. Tears clung to her eyelashes. "Oh, Drew, it looks wonderful." Without thinking, she threw her arms around him giving a giant hug. "I can't believe you guys did all of this work so fast." The smell of fresh cedar filled the space. "You replaced all of that rotten wood." She glanced up. "And the roof! This is incredible." Janie was overcome by the generosity of everyone who helped with the restoration. "I don't know how I'll ever repay all of you." She wiped her eyes.

"Come over this way," Drew motioned.

All of the stalls looked brand-new. "Was all of the wood replaced?" Janie ran her hand along the door.

"It sure was." Drew knocked on the side. "It's Tigerwood. Basically it's kick-proof lumber and low-maintenance. So, if you decide to get horses down the road, you're all set."

Overwhelmed, Janie took in her surroundings. "I planned on talking to you about horses—this is amazing!"

"Riley will love that. I do think having animals will be a big draw for the camp."

Janie agreed. Initially she only thought about the extra work, but the children could help with feeding the animals and cleaning the stalls. They'd have fun while developing a good work ethic. "I think so, too. Thank you for suggesting it."

"Did you notice that?" Drew pointed toward the loft.

"Oh my!" Janie ran to the brand-new cedar ladder and turned. "The kids will love this!" She quickly climbed to the top. "Look, there's even fresh hay. It smells so good." Janie peered down at Drew, smiling. A year ago, she'd been trapped in a horrible marriage, a relationship she never thought she'd escape. But she had. Now her life was so different. She was doing something that could have an impact on the lives of the children who visited the camp. Had God brought her home for this purpose? Or could He have even bigger plans for her? For the first time in a long time, Janie felt excited when she thought about the future.

Chapter Ten

Drew couldn't recall the last time he'd been this happy. Seeing Janie's reaction to the remodeled barn was something he'd never forget. Behind the wheel of his truck, he swallowed hard, sneaking glances her way while the two headed toward one of his favorite trails.

"It seems like a lifetime since I've hiked Rocky Gap," Janie said gazing out the window as the vehicle climbed the steep grade.

"Remember when we were teenagers and you begged me and Nick to take you along on your first hike?"

Janie laughed. "Don't even go there."

"What? You were the one who wore flip-flops. Nick and I tried to tell you that you needed to wear hiking boots, or at least tennis shoes." Drew remembered exactly what she'd worn that day and also how beautiful she had looked. In fact, he'd stumbled on a few roots because he had a hard time keeping his eyes off her.

"But the flip-flops went with my outfit." She nudged his arm. "I know. It was silly."

"You were so color-coordinated. Pink shorts, a pink-

and-white-striped T-shirt, a pink baseball hat and of course, those pink shoes."

"What can I say…I love the color." She paused and turned to him. "I can't believe you remember."

Drew eased the truck into a parking spot located near the base of the trail and looked at Janie. "I remember everything about that afternoon. It was the day I realized I kind of had a crush on you." His words surprised him. Had he really just confessed this secret he'd kept for years? Her cheeks blossomed in shades of red. "I'm sorry, Janie. I didn't mean to make you feel uncomfortable."

She unbuckled her seat belt and opened the car door before glancing over her shoulder at him. "You don't need to apologize. It's kind of funny actually because I had a major crush on you back then. Why do you think I wanted the perfect outfit?"

Janie jumped from the truck and closed the door, leaving him to digest that news.

A crush? He'd had no idea. Drew sat alone for a second and considered Janie's response. *Lord, have You orchestrated this reunion? Shaking his head, he followed her out of the truck and onto the trail.*

Forty-five minutes into the hike a sense of calmness had taken hold. This was why Drew hiked. Following the accident, these trails had become an escape from the guilt tethered around his brain. Hiking was his refuge. He slowed and turned to Janie. "Are you ready for a break or do you want to keep going?"

"Oh no, I feel great. Let's keep going."

Drew smiled. "The hiking boots make all the difference in the world, don't they?"

"Definitely." She laughed. "I can see why you love

it so much out here. I think it's great you can call this gorgeous sanctuary your office." Janie tripped on a root that crisscrossed the path.

"Careful now." Drew reached to steady her then stopped to take in his surroundings. "This place got me through the darkest days in my life. There were times I didn't think I'd survive." He paused to inhale a deep and steady breath. "I'd come out here and push myself to go that extra mile even though some days my legs felt like sacks of wet sand. The higher I went up the trail, the closer I felt to God."

Janie looked around. A squirrel scurried by and ran up a nearby tree trunk. "I can see why."

The sun filtered through the foliage, casting a radiant light on Janie's complexion. Drew felt safe with her. He always had. He could open up to her without judgment or criticism. "Sometimes I think I spend too much time out here. Too much time alone."

"Well, it's your job."

Drew agreed, but he was beginning to wonder if it was time to move on. "You're right, but even when I'm not working, I'm here. My friend Skip thinks I'm using the woods to hide from life."

"What do you think?" Janie questioned.

"He's probably right. At first, I needed to be here in order to work through my grief. But now, I think it's because I'm afraid to move on and start to live again." He'd never admitted that to anyone, and sharing it with Janie felt good. "Lately I've been thinking a lot about a goal I had—before the accident."

"I'd love to hear about it," Janie responded as their pace slowed.

Last night, when he'd been unable to sleep, Drew had

pulled out the box that contained his business plan and articles about similar businesses. "My wife and I had found a piece of property just outside Grayson's Gap. Working as a paramedic took me away from my family for long stretches, so I was looking for something that would allow me more time with them. We planned on building a home and opening a year-round outdoor adventure business with hikes, white-water rafting, horseback riding, snowboarding, cross-country skiing…you get the idea." Drew's adrenaline ticked up talking about it again. "We were even brainstorming names."

"I think that's a fantastic idea, Drew. There's nothing like it in the area, so I'm sure it would do well."

"That's what we thought, too. With all of the tourists passing through, we'd have a steady flow of patrons."

Janie's steps came to a halt. "Maybe it's time to renew that plan and go for it. You could use the land you're inheriting from Mrs. Applegate's estate."

It was as though she'd read his mind. "That's what I've been thinking about. I'm just not sure if I can do it on my own." He and his wife had planned to run their business as a team. She'd handle the financials since she had an accounting degree and Drew would run the business operations.

"I could help you," Janie offered.

"That's kind of you, but you've got enough on your plate right now. And honestly, I shouldn't even be talking about this until we get the camp up and running." Drew removed his backpack and pulled the zipper open, removing two bottles of water. "What do you say we drink these and hike up to the overlook? It's around two miles up."

"Sounds good." Janie took a long pull of her drink. "Just remember, the offer still stands."

With less than a mile to go, Drew was impressed by Janie's endurance. Without the flip-flops, she was a great hiker. Drew slowed his pace. "This part of the trail is a little tricky to navigate. Watch your footing and try not to get too close to the—"

Janie screamed as she slid down the embankment.

Drew's instincts took hold. He sprang into action and assessed the situation. A section of the trail narrowed. She'd stepped too close to the edge causing the ground beneath her boots to crumble. "Hang on, Janie," he called when he spotted her clinging to a large tree root. Beads of sweat peppered his forehead. She was only about ten feet down, but how long could she hold on?

More rocks fell when he stepped closer. He had to save her. Another life couldn't be lost on his watch. Drew flung his backpack to the ground. "Janie, just hang on. I'll get you! Hold on."

"I'm trying, but my arm…it hurts."

Drew struggled with the zipper on his bag. *Please Lord, let this rope be long enough to pull her back up to the trail.* He snatched the line and ran to the edge. "I'm going to drop this down to you. Make sure you get a firm grip on it and then I'll bring you up."

"Okay," she whimpered.

When he dropped the rope where she could reach it, a moment of relief settled in. "Okay, hold on to the tree root with one hand and grab the cord with the other. Try to favor that arm in case it's broken."

Drew watched Janie slowly extend her hand to the

rope. "That's it. Now grab it with the other. You're doing great, Janie. You'll be safe soon. Just hold on."

With slow and steady movements, Drew pulled. Janie moaned from below. Rocks tumbled down the mountainside as her body scraped against the ground.

"I don't think I can hold on any longer, Drew. My arm—it's not strong enough," she cried out.

"Yes you can, Janie! You're doing great. I've got you. I won't let you fall." He couldn't. Thoughts of his family raced through his mind. No. Not this time. With focus and intentional pulls Janie got closer. "Good job. You're almost there." Biting down on his lower lip, he drew his shoulders back and with one final pull, she was in his arms, lying on the ground. "You're safe… everything is okay."

Janie sat up and Drew followed her lead. "Thank you for saving my life, Drew. I don't know how I'll ever repay you." She threw her arms around him and buried her face into his chest. "All I could think about was Riley. What would happen to her?"

"Shh…don't think about that. You're safe now." He pulled back and gently brushed his hand across her cheek, wiping away the tears. "Do you want to go see Riley now?"

Janie nodded. "Yes…please. I need to see my daughter."

"Do you think you're okay to stand?" Drew watched Janie slowly get to her feet.

"I'm okay—it's just my arm," she said, running a hand over her left arm.

"Here, let me get your jacket off so I can take a look." He reached for her.

"No!" Janie jumped back with a start. "I'm fine. It's just strained." Her face reddened. "We need to go."

Drew didn't push it. As they headed down the path to the parking lot, Janie remained silent. Each time he glanced in her direction, she pulled on her sleeves while keeping her focus in front of her. What was it that she desperately tried to hide underneath the fabric?

Janie strolled along the sidewalk of downtown Whispering Slopes. Her arm felt back to normal after her fall during the hike with Drew. His quick instincts had saved her from being severely injured. She only wished she hadn't reacted so harshly when he wanted to check her arm. But what choice did she have? She couldn't risk him finding out about her past.

She squinted in the early morning sun and smiled. Janie loved the familiar shops. Memories of Saturday shopping trips with her mother flooded her mind. Before her mother became ill, they'd often spend the day hopping from shop to shop. Janie missed her shopping buddy. Her mother would have been a wonderful grandmother to Riley, if she hadn't gotten addicted to the pain medication.

Outside Buser's General Store Janie pulled open the door and the bell chimed. The scent of freshly baked muffins ignited her appetite, and her stomach grumbled.

"I'll be right with you," Mrs. Buser's sweet voice called out.

Janie breezed over to the baking aisle, picking up a basket along the way. The cake Drew had brought over for dinner the other evening had inspired Janie. She wanted to teach Riley how to make the homemade German chocolate cake using their family recipe passed down from generation to generation.

"Janie… How good to see you, dear." Mrs. Buser entered from the back office, gliding across the store.

The two embraced, then Mrs. Buser stepped back. "Where is that sweet little girl of yours?" She straightened her tight, gray bun.

Riley and Mrs. Buser had really bonded. When Janie picked Riley up after the hiking fiasco, she had talked nonstop about the fun she'd had working at the store. "I dropped her off at the library. They're having an all-day interactive computer class for children. Riley was so excited she got up at six o'clock this morning." Her daughter's interest in technology made her happy. Riley's school in Maryland believed in getting children working with computers as early as possible, and Riley was like a sponge, absorbing all of the knowledge she could. She'd even helped Janie out with the computer she'd purchased for the camp. "She loves anything high tech."

"That's wonderful. She is such a delightful child. We had so much fun the other day."

Janie nodded. "I know you did. Over dinner that night, she went on and on about all of the fun things she got to do here. Working the cash register was a highlight of the day."

"She's a quick study and a big help, too. If you ever need someone to watch her again, please send her over. I'll put her to work."

Janie laughed. "I'll keep that in mind, but you'll have to let me pay you."

"Nonsense. She's a good helper. I should put her on my payroll." Mrs. Buser removed the pencil nestled in her bun. "So what can I help you with today, sweetheart?"

"Well, I came in to get a few items to bake Riley's favorite cake."

"And what is that?" Mrs. Buser smiled.

"German chocolate."

The elderly woman rubbed her stomach. "Yum… that's my favorite, too."

"You'll have to come over for a slice. You'll love it. It's an old family recipe," Janie said picking up a package of flour and placing it inside the basket.

"Oh," Mrs. Buser licked her lips, "I'd love to. Family recipes passed down through generations are the best."

Once again, the sweet, sugary aroma tickled Janie's nose. "What kind of muffins are you making this morning? They smell divine."

Mrs. Buser reached for Janie's forearm and guided her to the counter. "I'm making chocolate chip with slices of almond."

"Yummy…I'll bet they are delicious." Janie's mouth watered.

"Have a seat. They're just about ready to come out of the oven and the coffee is brewing."

Mrs. Buser scurried back to the kitchen. The store hadn't changed since Janie lived here. Just like One More Scoop, it was a place to relax and hang out. With the expansive counter, you could grab a bite to eat or a cup of coffee before or after you shopped. What Janie had always loved most about Buser's General Store was how everyone knew one another. She found that comforting. Janie's shoulders relaxed as she gazed around the quaint store. This town was where she and Riley belonged.

Moments later, Mrs. Buser returned carrying a tray with one coffee cup and a plump, oversize muffin.

"Aren't you going to join me?" Janie asked, eyeing the treat big enough for two. "I don't think I can eat that by myself."

Mrs. Buser placed the tray on the counter, removing the items and setting them in front of Janie. She rubbed her hands across her waistline that was outfitted with a red apron. "Oh no, my days of enjoying goodies have passed. I can't allow these apron strings to get any tighter. You're young. You have plenty of time to eat whatever you'd like, so enjoy."

Janie pinched off a nugget of the warm muffin, then popped it in her mouth. "Yum…this is pure decadence. It's melting away on my tongue."

The woman smiled. "These are made from my great-grandmother's recipe. She left behind so many, I always thought I'd like to publish a cookbook that contained all of her delicious food and desserts."

"Maybe you should. This is too wonderful to keep to yourself." Janie licked some chocolate from her finger, savoring every morsel. "Self-publishing is always an option."

Mrs. Buser pulled a blue-and-white dish towel from behind the counter and wiped the already spotless top. "Maybe I will. So tell me, are you and Drew ready for the big grand opening?"

For the first time since learning about her inheritance, her stomach didn't turn upside down at the mention of the camp. Thanks to Drew and so many of the locals, she was confident things would run smooth on their first day. "If you asked me a week ago, I would have been honest and told you I was a nervous wreck."

"And now?" The woman leaned over the counter.

"I'm so excited. I can hardly wait much longer. Hopefully the weather will cooperate." She'd been monitoring the long-range forecast even though it wasn't always predictable. She had to pray and trust God to provide a picture-perfect day.

"Let me know if there's anything I can do to help. Riley seems to be over the moon about the opening." Mrs. Buser paused and passed a serious look at Janie. "You know, she's quite smitten with Drew. She talks nonstop about him."

Janie had mixed feelings about her daughter's attachment to Drew. "Do you think it's healthy for her to feel that way?" Janie hadn't planned on sharing her marital problems with Mrs. Buser, but the woman had always been wise. "Her father and I divorced after ten years of marriage. During the proceedings, he never tried to obtain custody or even visitation rights," she added.

Mrs. Buser shook her head. "How could anyone walk away from such a delightful child?"

"I think he did it because he knew it would hurt me. Even though our marriage is over, he's intent on causing me more pain." Janie stopped short of sharing the physical pain that she'd survived during her marriage. Why had she stayed so long?

"You might be right. It's only natural for Riley to feel the way she does about Drew, though. He's a good man who has suffered loss himself. Maybe they're connecting through their mutual losses."

Could that be true? Drew lost his child and Riley lost her father. Were they filling a void for one another? "Drew recently told me about the accident."

The door chimed as a customer entered the store, and Mrs. Buser turned. "Good morning, Jonathan. Let me know if I can help you with anything."

The local nodded and went in search of his groceries.

Mrs. Buser continued, "The accident just about devastated him. When he left his paramedic position and went into seclusion at his cabin, the entire town was worried sick about him. He'd been such a wonderful husband and father. To lose his beautiful family so tragically... I didn't think he'd ever work through his grief."

"He seems to be handling it now. Don't you think?"

"Yes, I think so." The woman hesitated. "Funny, since you've come back, Drew seems to be doing better than I've seen him in the last two years. I believe you and Riley are good for him."

Janie was caught off guard by her friend's words. Maybe her daughter was good for Drew, but Janie questioned whether or not she herself would ever be good for any man. Her ex-husband sure didn't think so. Up until the day they divorced, he made sure he reminded her how weak and worthless she was. As much as she'd been enjoying the time spent with Drew, she knew she wasn't wife material.

Chapter Eleven

The July Fourth sun burst through a layer of cumulus clouds like a firecracker as Drew watched Janie and Riley climb out of her vehicle.

"Can you believe this day has finally arrived?" Janie was beaming. "And look," she pointed, "the sun is finally out!"

The couple had agreed to meet at the farm bright and early on opening day. They had three hours before the gates opened. Drew had spent the last two days posting signs to advertise the grand reopening all around Whispering Slopes and neighboring towns. He looked down at Riley. "Hey, munchkin." He patted the top of her head. "Thanks for all of the online shout-outs you did."

Riley smiled. "Mrs. Cathcart from the library helped. When I was there last Saturday, she worked with me to set up a Twitter page for the camp. She used to spend her summers there, too, so she had a lot of old pictures. We have over one thousand followers already!" Riley announced. "I'm going to go help Mrs. Buser in the activity building. Is that okay, Mommy?"

Janie nodded. "Okay, but tell her if she needs anything to let me know."

"I will!" Riley yelled over her shoulder as she took off toward the building.

Janie turned to Drew. "I didn't think I'd ever get her to sleep last night. She was so excited."

"I had a little trouble falling asleep myself." Drew scratched the top of his head. "That's pretty impressive about the Twitter following, but do you think it's wise for a seven-year-old to have a social media account?"

Janie laughed. "This is all Lisa Cathcart's doing. Riley only observed and helped with the photographs to go along with the Tweets. Lisa had called to offer her support and suggested the idea. She used to help Mrs. Applegate with the camp."

Drew remembered Lisa's efforts to keep the camp open after Mr. Applegate had passed away. "We might have a bigger crowd than we anticipated. It's going to be a long day. Are you ready for it?"

Janie looked around, then turned to Drew. "I guess I have to be, right? Thank you so much for all of your help. Because of you, Riley and I will have a good life here in Whispering Slopes." She rested her hand on his arm.

"I can't take all of the credit. A lot of people in this town worked together. They care about you and Riley." And with each passing day, he was caring more for them.

Janie wiped the tear that trickled down her cheek. "The support has been overwhelming."

Drew stepped closer and reached for her hand. "Remember, Janie, you worked hard, too. You have to take some of the credit."

She nodded.

Janie's self-esteem wasn't like Drew remembered. She seemed so unsure of herself, constantly second-guessing her moves. He could only hope running this camp would rebuild her confidence.

"The past few weeks have gone so fast. I imagine you're anxious to return to work. Back to the seclusion you crave."

Drew had been thinking a lot about his duties at the park. He'd started to question whether God was nudging him in another direction. Spending time with Janie and Riley, along with the townspeople, had him second-guessing his own future. Did he want to live the remaining days of his life alone? Like his buddy Skip had told him, it wasn't what Lori would have wanted for him. A part of him dreaded returning to work. *Just say it.* "Actually, I'm not looking forward to it. I've thought a lot more about the outdoor adventure company."

"And?" A hint of hopefulness sounded in Janie's voice.

Was this his second chance? How could he not go for it? "Last night I started to think about new names for my outdoor adventure business." There. He said it. What's that saying? A dream isn't real until it's spoken, or something like that.

Janie squealed. "This is so exciting! I'm really happy for you, Drew. Remember what I said—I'll help you in any way I can." She paused for a moment before continuing. "In fact, what if I offered to be your business partner in this venture?"

Drew shuffled back a step. Going into a partnership was one thing, but with Janie? How could he keep his heart protected if he formed a lifelong business relationship? Then again, he did need some financial backing, which would require him to take out a loan. He'd never borrowed money in his life. Did he really want to start now? Was this God's plan for him?

"Drew? What do you say? Would you like a partner? We could combine the two businesses."

Drew responded, "Rocky River Camp and Outdoor Adventures…it does have a nice ring to it." He smiled. "Can I think about it?"

Janie jumped up and down, clapping her hands. Two doves perched on a nearby red spruce branch cooed and took flight. "I'm so excited! It could be really great to have the camp and the adventure center as one operation. There's nothing like it anywhere in the area."

"Well, first we have to get this camp open for our guests and for Mrs. Applegate. Let's grab Riley and head down to the barn. Joe Simpson and his friend will be here any minute with the two horses and the goats," Drew explained. He'd been pleased when Janie had agreed that adding more animals to the farm would only benefit the camp in the long run.

"Riley is so excited."

Drew couldn't wait to see her reaction. "Even more so when we tell her she gets to name all of her new critters." He winked.

"They're here, they're here!" Riley squealed like a baby piglet wanting free from its pen when Joe's truck and trailer barreled down the gravel road, leaving a cloud of dust in its path thirty minutes later.

"Have you thought of any names, Riley?" Drew asked.

Riley placed her hands on her hips, crinkling her nose. "I need to see them first. You can't give something or someone a name without seeing their face, Mr. Drew."

Janie and Drew shared a laugh. "I guess you're right."

After the truck pulled up in front of the barn, Joe exited the vehicle. "Good morning, Drew. This is my buddy George." He gestured to the man as George joined them.

Drew shook Joe's hand, then stepped toward George. "It's a pleasure to meet you. This is Janie and her daughter Riley."

"Pleasure to meet you," Joe said while George nodded.

"Thanks for bringing over the animals." Janie smiled.

"Yeah, I can't wait to meet them," Riley cheered. "Tonight I'm going to call all of my old friends from Maryland and tell them about my new pets."

Drew's heart soared when the little girl's face lit up as George led one of the horses off the trailer. "This one is a male and Joe has the other. It's a female."

"This is exactly what I thought Buddy would look like!" Riley yelled.

Drew glanced in Janie's direction and winked.

As Joe led the female out of the trailer, Janie looked down at her daughter. "Did you have a name for her?"

Riley ran toward the horse and gave it a closer inspection. "That's Brandy!"

Drew nodded. "Buddy and Brandy. I like it. Great choices, munchkin."

Minutes later with the horses housed in their new stalls, Drew turned to Riley. "Are you ready to name the goats?"

Riley rapidly nodded her head up and down without saying a word.

Janie gasped when Joe and George each lead a baby goat on a red leash. "They're so adorable."

The men approached Riley. She dropped to her knees, giving each goat a giant bear hug.

"These fellas are brother and sister. That's the girl," Joe pointed to the white one with brown markings, "and this brown one is a boy."

"Riley, it's your call again," Drew instructed.

"I want to name the girl Fiona and the boy Phillip," Riley answered without hesitation.

Drew thought Phillip was a little unusual for a goat, but it's what Riley wanted.

"How did you come up with that name for the boy?" Janie lowered her gaze to her daughter.

Riley shrugged her shoulders. "I don't know. It just popped into my head."

All of the adults shared a laugh. "By the way, all of the animals were fed this morning, so you won't have to worry about them until this evening," Joe said.

"What about their lunch?" Riley tugged on Joe's arm.

"They'll graze on grass throughout the day." He patted her head. "Don't worry—they'll be fine."

Janie paid Joe for the animals, and he and George headed to his truck. "Wishing you the best," Joe called out the window as the men drove off down the road.

Janie looked at Drew and ran her hand across her forehead. "I had no idea horses were so expensive. It's a good thing Mrs. Applegate thought ahead to provide me with start-up money in her will. I would have never been able to afford this."

"She had a good head for business." Drew checked his watch. "We've got over an hour before the gates open. Let's walk down to the activity building and make sure Mrs. Buser is on schedule with the food."

Moments later, the three entered the building. A smoky haze coated the room.

"Why is it so smoky in here?" Riley shouted. "Is something burning?"

Drew ran into the kitchen. Thick black smoke burned his eyes. "Mrs. Buser! Are you here?" He ran toward the oversize oven where smoke billowed. After turning it off, he reached for the pot holders then flung open the oven door. Grabbing the large baking pan with his covered hands, he tossed it into the sink before reaching inside for the second charred dish.

"Be careful, Drew! Don't burn yourself," Janie cried out.

"Where's Mrs. Buser, Mommy?"

Drew turned on the water, allowing it to rush over the meat to stop it from smoking.

"Oh my! What happened?" Mrs. Buser bustled into the kitchen through the back door carrying her cell phone.

Drew reached for the spigot to turn off the water. "Well, we were kind of wondering the same thing."

"My daughter called from Colorado. The connection wasn't good in here, so I stepped outside. I was only gone for a few minutes." She glanced toward the charred chicken tossed in the sink. "What in the world? I turned the oven to low before I went outdoors."

After walking toward the oven, Drew checked the temperature. "It's set on five hundred degrees."

"Oh no!" Mrs. Buser covered her mouth with her right hand. "I must have turned the knob in the wrong direction. I'm so sorry." Tears pooled in her eyes.

Drew's stomach twisted. He'd made her cry. That was the last thing he wanted to do. He slowly approached her and rested his hand on her arm. "Don't worry about it. You made an honest mistake."

"But today is your grand opening. I've ruined everything." She pulled a tissue from her apron pocket and blotted her eyes.

Janie approached. "Mrs. Buser, please calm down. Everything will be okay. Accidents happen."

Drew opened the back door and then hurried to the window over the sink to allow the warm summer breeze inside. "Janie's right. No harm done. Once the place airs out it will be fine."

"But what about the food? We won't have any lunch for the guests." Mrs. Buser eyed the sink.

"Don't worry about that. I'll run out to the grocery store and pick up some hamburger meat and hot dogs. We can fire up the grill outside. It's summertime. We should be cooking outdoors anyway." Drew double-checked his watch. "We've got plenty of time. I'll be right back."

"Can I go with Mr. Drew, Mommy?" Riley asked, looking toward Janie and then back to Drew. "I can show him the kind of buns we like best."

Janie turned to Drew.

"Sure, come on, munchkin. We need to get moving." Drew fished his car keys from his pocket.

"Janie and I will finish cleaning up and then we'll set up the tables outside. It's a beautiful day for outdoor dining," Mrs. Buser announced, the kitchen fiasco obviously already forgotten.

Drew stepped outside, inhaling the fresh air.

"It smells better out here, doesn't it?" Riley looked up and giggled.

"It sure does."

As the two walked toward the car, Riley reached for Drew's hand. His chest tightened. Images of Heidi raced through his mind. He could hardly breathe. Could he handle going into partnership with Janie? Maybe he was getting in over his head. He'd be spending a lot of time with Janie and constantly fighting his attraction. Then there was Riley—a reminder of his daughter. When they arrived at the vehicle, he pulled his hand from hers. He could finally breathe again.

Three hours after the camp opened, the little mishap in the activity building was long forgotten. Standing near the grill, Janie took in her surroundings. Never in her wildest dreams did she expect such a big turnout on their opening day, though she'd prayed for it. Today she was blessed with more children and parents than she ever thought possible. She approached Drew, who was busy grilling onions. "Are we going to have enough food for all of these people? This is unbelievable."

Drew laughed. "We should be okay, but you're right. Where did all of these kids come from?"

Janie stepped to the side when the smoke from the grill blew in her direction. "I guess all of the advertising has paid off. I've been talking to a few parents from neighboring counties. They don't have anything like our camp. When I mentioned the outdoor adventure addition there was a lot of interest. I think your idea would be a big hit."

When Drew didn't respond, curiosity got the best of her. "Why are you so quiet? I thought you'd be happy about this."

Drew removed the onions wrapped in tinfoil from the grill and placed them on a plate. "I'm thrilled the camp is having a successful opening day, but I suppose I'm having some second thoughts about the whole outdoor thing."

To say she was disappointed would be an understatement. "Look around you. How could you second-guess your idea? We'd have to turn kids away. This is exactly the type of thing our community needs. It's obvious neighboring towns lack in entertainment for kids."

"I agree with everything you're saying, Janie."

What was going on with him? "Then why have you had a change of heart? I don't understand."

"I don't know if it's a good idea for us to work so closely together," he admitted.

"Why would that be a problem? Look at what we accomplished getting ready for today. We make a great team." She paused before speaking again. "At least I thought we did." Janie grew uneasy with Drew's sudden turnaround.

"We did—I mean, we do. Yes, I agree with you. It's just—" He raked his hand through his hair.

"Is it Riley?" Was she being insensitive? Putting her own wants and needs before Drew's feelings. Seeing Riley every day couldn't be easy. "I can do some juggling with her schedule so she's not around you so much."

Drew shook his head and picked up the serving dish containing rows of hamburger patties and hot dogs. "That wouldn't be fair to her, or to you. She's excited about the camp and running it with you is something that will make her happy." One by one, he placed the burgers on the grill, and sizzling sounds erupted as flames danced around the grease.

Janie's stomach rumbled at the tantalizing aroma

of the food. "But what about you? I want you to have your dream. After everything you've been through, you deserve it."

Drew picked up the spatula and flipped the burgers. "As hard as it's been for me to be around Riley, I think she's helped me to cope with my loss." He hesitated. "And maybe I'm helping her, too, by filling the void left when you and her father divorced."

Janie wouldn't admit it to Drew, but he was right. Since meeting him, Riley had dropped several hints about Drew making a good father. And he would, but it frightened her. Janie couldn't bear to see her daughter hurt again. "I'm happy that she's helped you, Drew."

"Just the people I was looking for." Janie whirled around to the deep, raspy voice approaching from behind.

"Mr. Mayor." Drew gave a nod to the short and portly man. "Sir, this is Janie Edmiston. She lived in Whispering Slopes when she was younger. She recently moved back with her daughter."

The mayor extended his hand. "I've heard a lot of good things about you from Elsie Buser."

"It's nice to meet you, sir." Janie accepted the firm handshake.

"Why were you looking for us?" Drew asked the mayor.

He cleared his throat. "Two reasons, actually. First, I wanted to congratulate both of you on the reopening. I know Mrs. Applegate would be proud of the work you've put into bringing her dream back to life. This camp is such a big part of Whispering Slopes' history. I'm thrilled to see such a big turnout today."

The mayor's words caused a lump to form in Janie's

throat. She missed her dear friend and wished she could be here with them to celebrate. "Thank you so much for your kind words, Mr. Mayor."

"Please, call me Ben."

"Ben." Her lashes were damp with tears. "Mrs. Applegate touched so many lives. Growing up, she was like a mother to me. Keeping this camp open to honor her memory is the least I can do." She'd never forget everything Mrs. Applegate had done for her. Even now, she continued to make a better life for her and Riley.

"You both have done an outstanding job. You work well together. That leads me to the second item I wanted to speak with you about." Ben eyed the hamburgers sizzling on the grill. "I was thrilled to hear about the outdoor adventure business the two of you plan to open. There's been a lot of buzz and excitement."

"Boy, word really does get around in a small town, doesn't it?" Drew laughed.

Janie spoke up. "I'm afraid that's my doing, Drew. After you told me about your idea, I was so excited—maybe too excited. I shared the news with a few parents and Mrs. Buser."

"I see."

Judging by his response, Janie couldn't tell if he was upset with her. "I'm sorry. It wasn't my news to share."

Ben turned his focus on Drew who was busy flipping the burgers. "Don't be upset with her. She might have done you and all of us a big favor."

"How so?" Drew questioned.

Ben stepped a little closer, checked his surroundings and lowered his voice. "Let's be honest here. We all know Mrs. Buser can—well, you know…talk. I always say to my wife, if you want something to be known around town, tell Mrs. Buser. Bless her heart. Anyway, she's already called her connections at all of the newspapers and news channels in the area to arrange for you two to do interviews for the paper and on the local news. Isn't that great?"

Janie's stomach flipped. What had she done? While Drew was reconsidering going forward with his new business, Mrs. Buser was out marketing to the entire state. How could she fix this mess?

"So?" Ben looked at Drew, then Janie. "What do you guys think?"

"Well—"

"No, Drew, let me explain," Janie interrupted Drew, then mouthed "I'm sorry" before turning to Ben. "I'm afraid I jumped the gun in discussing the adventure center with Mrs. Buser. Earlier, when Drew told me about it, he was only considering it."

Ben looked at Drew with his brow arched. "Is that true, son?"

"Yes, sir."

"Well, what can I do to help convince you that your idea would be the best thing to happen to Whispering Slopes in a long time? If money is an issue, I'm sure we can get some help from the community," the man offered.

Drew grabbed a clean plate from the nearby picnic table. "We've got a lot of hungry people here today. I better get these hamburgers off the grill and throw on the hot dogs. Can I think about it some more?"

"Of course. I didn't mean to come over here and pressure you, Drew. I was so thrilled to hear about your plans. I suppose I got a little carried away, too. You enjoy today and take your time making a decision. I'll tell Mrs. Buser to hold off with the press." He patted Drew's shoulder. "Now, how about one of those burgers? I'm starving."

Wearing a big smile, Ben headed off for a place to sit down to enjoy his meal. Janie spun around on her heel. "I'm so sorry, Drew. I should have never opened my big mouth to Mrs. Buser. I had no idea she'd call the media."

Drew removed the last hamburger from the grill. A smile parted his lips as he gazed over the crowd of excited guests. "It's not your fault. This is probably the nudge that I need to move on and put the past behind me. Plus, we can't let all of these people down now, can we? Besides, how can we fail when we've got a one-woman marketing team like Mrs. Buser in our corner?" He placed the platter on the grill side table and reached out his hand. "Do you want to shake on it—partner?"

Janie's face felt warm as Drew held her hand. A tingling sensation shot up her arm. Her reaction surprised her. Stunned her was more like it. Yes, she'd had feelings for him when she was younger. But that was all in the past. Wasn't it? It had to be if they were going to be working so closely together. She couldn't allow her heart to weaken and risk her secret being exposed. *Business partners.* That's all they could be—all they could ever be.

Chapter Twelve

The blaring alarm clock jarred Drew from a deep sleep. Reaching over, he pressed his hand on the button and rolled onto his back. He couldn't remember the last time he'd had such a peaceful night of rest.

He stared at the ceiling. Today was the day. Excitement coursed through his veins in anticipation of the day's schedule. First, an appointment with the attorney to pick up the deed to the land left to him by Mrs. Applegate. After, he planned to meet with Janie and Larry to set up the partnership agreement for the sports center.

Six days had passed since the opening of the camp and Drew's discussion with the mayor. During that time, he'd gone to his special place and prayed each morning. On the third day, he'd given notice to his employer before making a call to the mayor to let him know his decision. There was no turning back now.

Padding into the kitchen, he flipped the switch on the coffee maker before taking a seat at the table. As he fired up his laptop, the aroma of fresh brew filled the air. He pulled up the *Whispering Slopes Times* website and smiled at the article filling the front page, along with an oversize photograph of the mayor. A lengthy story announced the plans to open Rocky River Camp and Outdoor Adventures. The paper had also posted a picture taken of Drew and Janie at the camp opening. There was no turning back. Their partnership was now official. When the coffee maker beeped, Drew rose from the table to begin his day.

Later that morning, Drew turned into the parking lot of his attorney's office and spotted Janie's car. He strolled through the lot, removing his sunglasses when he reached the door. Upon entering, he blinked several times in the dark room, wondering if his eyes were adjusting from coming in out of the bright sunlight. He blinked again. No. The lights were definitely off in the suite. "Hello? Is anyone here?" The front desk was empty, but he heard noises coming from down the hall. "Larry?"

Janie entered the reception area holding a cup of coffee. "Hello, Drew." She smiled, taking a quick sip.

"Did Larry forget to pay his electric bill?" Drew joked.

"Oh no. He said they lost power from the storm last night. The power company said it would be back on by nine o'clock this morning." She glanced at her watch. "Obviously they've underestimated their repair time."

Drew looked around the room. "Where's the munchkin?"

"She's helping Mrs. Buser with the store. I told her I'd pick her up when we're done and we'd go over to our new home before Laura Marie and Mark take the kids on their nature hike." Janie smiled and released a slow breath. "I can't believe I'm even saying that—our new home. It hasn't quite sunk in yet."

"It will once you're settled." Drew was thrilled for Janie and Riley. "Mark and Laura Marie were great hires." When the director from the community college in Grayson's Gap called with two recommendations, both forestry majors, the decision was easy.

Janie nodded. "You're not kidding. They're great with the kids."

Drew made a mental note to call the school. Maybe they'd have a few more referrals for the new business. "Do you want me to come with you to the house? I can take care of some of the minor repairs. It shouldn't take too long. Then we can head to the camp together. I'd like to run a few ideas past Laura Marie and Mark."

Drew noticed Janie's shoulders relax before she answered. "I was hoping you'd offer to come over, Drew. I'm a little nervous. I've never owned a home."

"This isn't a time for worrying, Janie. You should be celebrating the start of your new life."

"Hello, Drew." Larry Caldwell entered the room. "Sorry about the electrical issues. We can still take care of the deed and draw up the partnership agreement, but you'll have to wait on copies of the documents."

"Good to see you." Drew extended his hand to his lawyer. "No worries on the paperwork. I just hope you're not left in the dark all day. That was some storm we had last night. I saw some downed power lines on the way over."

"Let's step into the conference room and get started. There's more daylight in there." Larry chuckled. "By the way—" he glanced at Janie "—your funds have been wired into your account. If you'd like the name of a good investor, let me know. Oh, and Drew, after our discussion about your timeline for opening, I planned to put the fifteenth of August into the agreement," he added. "Is that okay?"

Drew turned to Janie and she nodded. "That works for us, sir," he answered.

The three walked down the hall and into the conference room. Drew considered Janie. So much had changed since they'd first reconnected at the reading of Mrs. Applegate's will. Today she was the owner of a lovely home and potentially a successful camp and outdoor adventure facility. If she invested wisely, she'd have enough money to provide a comfortable life for her and her daughter. Now she was officially committing to becoming Drew's business partner. A lot was changing for him, as well. With help from Janie, he was excited to see the dream he and his wife once had come to life.

Forty minutes later, Drew pulled up in front of Janie and Riley's new home. How many laps had he run around the wraparound porch as a child? The house held a lot of memories for many who'd grown up in Whispering Slopes. Mr. and Mrs. Applegate were loved by the community. Drew knew Janie would be as welcoming as the previous owners. He'd watched her interact with the kids since the camp opened, and she was great with them. He only hoped he could follow her lead. Being around Riley was one thing, but he found it more of a struggle with a larger group of kids. Of course, he'd have to get over it and the sooner the better.

Placing the car into Park, Drew exited the vehicle, pocketing his keys. He sauntered toward the house. His shoes crunched on the gravel driveway until he reached the cement sidewalk leading to the porch steps. He took a seat and looked out on to the property, shading his eyes from the bright July sun as the cicadas buzzed.

Although the camp wasn't visible from the porch, in the distance Drew heard the sound of children's laughter carrying across the rolling fields that surrounded the house.

When his phone chimed, he removed it from his back pocket and read the incoming text message reminding him of his meeting tomorrow with the architect. Drew had sent him some rough ideas for the main sports facility and tomorrow he'd see the plans. Thing were moving along quickly.

A car traveling over the rocks took Drew's eyes off his phone. A black sedan with tinted windows stirred up dust as it approached. Drew stood, squinting at the vehicle, unable to see the driver. The car came to an abrupt stop. A second later, it accelerated and made a rapid U-turn off the driveway and into the grass before it sped from the house. *Strange.*

Drew scratched his head as he remembered the bold house number on the mailbox along the roadside. He shrugged his shoulders. Maybe they'd missed it and mistakenly turned down the wrong driveway. But something didn't feel right.

"Thanks for fixing the leak under the kitchen sink, earlier." Janie's fingers tapped out numbers on the keyboard.

She loved the office she'd set up for her and Drew in the activity building. They each had their own matching maple desks that faced separate windows. Their backs were to each other in order to maintain a little privacy. A large lateral file cabinet with framed photos of Riley on top lined the wall near the door. A brown-

and-cream-colored oriental rug covered the center of the tiled floor.

At first she didn't think sharing an office would be a good idea. Lately, being in close proximity to Drew had her thinking about what could have been. But she couldn't venture down that path. She had a new business to get off the ground and a daughter to care for. There was no time to give her heart to another man. Besides, what was the point? She'd learned the hard way that romantic love equals pain. Janie was determined to think with her head and not her heart.

"No problem. The sink was an easy fix." Drew swiveled his chair around to face Janie. "You're really fast on that." He pointed to the computer.

Janie considered Drew's remark. Her ex-husband used to tell her she must not know how to operate a computer judging by all of the mathematical errors she made in their checkbook. Two months into their marriage, he'd taken over all of their finances. He changed the passwords on the online bank accounts as well as their investments. He'd taken control of everything... including her life.

Shaking away the thoughts, she laughed. "Over ten years ago, when I was first married, I briefly worked in an office. Over time, I got faster and faster."

"How come you only worked there for a short amount of time?" Drew stretched back in his chair, swinging his gaze in her direction.

Pulling her hand from her work, she massaged her right temple with her fingertip. For a second, Janie thought about sharing her past with Drew, but what would be the point? Either he'd feel sorry for her or he'd think she was a fool for staying in the marriage as long as she had. If she was going to move on with her life, then all of the pain that went along with the past needed to be buried. Talking about it would only re-open wounds that she'd tried so hard to mend. Though some days, it felt like a losing battle. "We decided we wanted to try to start a family," she responded, hoping he'd move on to another topic.

"So you didn't want to be one of those do-it-all moms?"

Her stomach twisted. Why was he so curious about her past? "No, my husband thought it was best for me— for Riley, if I stayed home to be a full-time mother." Janie observed Drew's left brow arch.

"So you didn't get a say in the matter?"

Janie shrugged. "I didn't bring in the income to jus-tify the day care expense."

Silence lingered until the air-conditioning powered on. The thermostat was kept low and made their office quite cold. Janie was happy she didn't need to make up any excuse for keeping her jacket on. "Let me finish this and if you're ready, the kids should be returning from their hike. I can take them to the cafeteria if you'd like to speak with Mark and Laura Marie." She turned back to her work and Drew did the same.

A short time later, with the administrative duties complete, Janie and Drew headed outside to meet up with the children. A warm breeze danced in the air.

"It feels good to get out of that cold office." Drew stretched his arms overhead.

"Mr. Drew!"

Janie whirled toward her daughter's voice. Riley raced down the path to the clearing. She couldn't get to Drew fast enough. Janie's heart tugged at the sight of Riley flying into his arms and Drew spinning her around like she was on a carnival ride. The feelings bubbling in Janie's heart were conflicting. She was angry at her ex-husband, yet drawn to Drew's kindness. His gentle ways were helping her daughter cope with the reality that her father had disowned his child just to get back at her mother.

"I'm getting dizzy!" Riley giggled as she whirled through the air.

Drew placed her on the ground and she staggered toward her mother.

"Did you have a good time on the hike?" Janie brushed her daughter's hair away from her eyes.

"It was great! Mark and Laura Marie let us stick our feet in the river," Riley cheered.

Drew looked down at the little girl. "Did you get your shoes wet?"

Riley giggled. "No, we took them off, silly."

Janie glanced in Drew's direction. He winked, causing her heart to flutter. This was happening more often. She couldn't help it. The way Drew treated Riley was so endearing.

"Mommy, the next time we go, you and Mr. Drew should come, too. It was so much fun. We even saw a couple of snakes, but Mark said they weren't poisonous."

"Don't forget, munchkin, on Monday a group of us will be going horseback riding," Drew explained.

Janie spoke up. "Well, if Mr. Harp delivers our ten new horses today." She couldn't believe how fast the farm was growing. When they lived in Maryland, they never had any pets. Her ex-husband claimed he was allergic to all animals. Janie never believed him. He just didn't want to be bothered by them, let alone the cost of caring for them.

"I can't believe we're going to have twelve horses," Riley sang out, jumping up and down. "I love my life!"

Janie couldn't have been happier. When she finally had the nerve to leave her husband and Maryland, she had been filled with so much doubt, but hearing her daughter say those words confirmed what she'd hoped was true. Whispering Slopes was exactly where God wanted them to be. She looked at Drew, who stood smiling. "I love my life, too," Janie agreed and her eyes connected with Drew's. A shy smile curved his lips.

He spoke, breaking her trance. "We need to purchase the saddles before Monday."

Janie's body tensed. "I completely forgot. Can we order them and expedite the delivery?"

Drew laughed. "Saddlers don't work like online stores."

Janie's face warmed. "I guess I have a lot to learn." She bit her lower lip. The money for the riding tour scheduled for Monday had been prepaid. Drew had been right when he suggested adding horses to the farm. Horseback riding was already generating a substantial amount of income. "So what can we do? We can't have our guests riding bareback."

"I thought I'd take a road trip to Lexington tomorrow and visit Lexington's Heritage. The owner, Shane McWilliams, has been in the business for years. He's a good and honest businessman. He'll give us the best prices."

"Would you like some company?" What was she thinking? "I mean—you shouldn't have to do all of the work. I know we agreed to split the costs of the horses since we'll use them for the outdoor center as well, but your time is valuable."

Drew flashed a smile. "Hey, you don't need to convince me. We can bring the munchkin, too," he said pointing over to Riley who was picking honeysuckle.

"She's working with Mrs. Buser tomorrow," Janie responded. For a second, a twinge of excitement coursed through her at the thought of being alone with Drew. But it passed. Time away from the farm could result in more questions from him about her past.

"Great. I'll swing by and pick you up around nine o'clock, if that works for you."

After Drew went to meet up with Mark and Laura Marie, Janie tried to shake off the warm and fuzzy feelings that seemed to be happening more frequently in Drew's presence. If their partnership was going to be successful, she needed to keep her mind on the business and off Drew. But she had to admit, it was becoming more and more difficult. And now she'd committed to a road trip with him.

Later, following a quick bite of lunch, Janie went back to the office to finish up some paperwork. Riley stayed behind to help the volunteers get the stalls ready for the new horses.

Three yawns in a row drove Janie from her chair and straight to the coffee maker. Last night's storm had kept her awake for most of the night as the thunder continued to rumble for hours. When it had finally stopped, she'd been wide-awake. Grabbing a filter from the overhead cabinet, she opened the can of grounds and scooped out five heaping spoons. Thinking about the piles of paperwork she needed to plough through today, she tossed in an extra scoop.

When her phone chimed, she finished pouring the water into the reservoir and flipped the switch to On before walking back to her desk to check the device. Her stomach rolled over when she opened her email and spotted her ex-husband's address in her inbox. Her finger hovered over the Delete button. There was nothing he could say that she'd have any interest in hearing. Then she thought of Riley. No matter how much pain Randy had caused, they did have a child together. What if something had happened to one of his parents? Riley loved her grandparents.

She clicked open the email, read the content and shivered. No salutation and no signature, but one strong message that read, I want to see my daughter.

It had been him—that day at the carnival. At the time, she hoped she'd been wrong, but she hadn't imagined it. He was in her town, or at least he had been. Was this email sent from Maryland? Or was he still in Whispering Slopes? She had no way of knowing unless she opened the line of communication by responding to his email.

Minutes later, still staring at the screen, Janie jumped when the coffee maker beeped. Suddenly her safe little town felt far from secure. She wanted to hit Delete and pretend he'd never tried to contract her, but that would make him mad. When he got angry, he was capable of anything. She had the scars to prove it. Scrolling through her contacts, she pulled up her divorce attorney's information. She'd make a quick call to Maryland to find out the best way to handle Randy.

Following a ten-minute conversation with her lawyer, Ted Forbes, Janie had her answer—if Randy wanted visitation rights, he'd need to go through his attorney.

Her lawyer also advised her to keep her reply short. After telling him to contact his attorney, Ted said it would be best if she had no further communication with him. He reminded her about Randy's past behavior. She almost laughed. He didn't need to tell her that. She was fully aware.

Her fingers trembled as she typed her response and hit Send. Within a couple of seconds, her phone indicated another email. The second message had a subject line that read, Don't delete me! Without reading it, she immediately swiped away the correspondence. Her attorney had been right about ceasing communication with Randy. But this would make him angry. As long as she'd known him, he'd never taken no for an answer. He always had to have the last word.

Chapter Thirteen

Drew slid his hands inside the pockets of his boot-cut jeans, before taking the front steps of Janie's house two at a time. The idea of spending the day with her had him feeling like a teenager. Since she'd moved back to Whispering Slopes, they'd had little time alone.

Drew smiled as he reached the door. When he and some of the guys from town helped Janie move into her new home, Janie had mentioned to Drew that she'd always wanted a red front door. This morning he'd gone to the hardware store and purchased the paint. Another project he'd add to his list. Three knocks told him she wasn't inside. Glancing at his watch, Drew realized he was early. With Janie nowhere in sight, he headed to the stalls.

Once outside the structure he peeked in through the open door and his heart skipped a beat. Dressed in jeans and a long-sleeved white sweatshirt with her hair pulled back into a loose ponytail, Janie sat on the floor of the stall with Fiona and Phillip climbing all over her. Laughter filled the area.

"I had a feeling I'd find you down here." Drew stepped inside.

Janie jumped and Buddy bounded toward Drew. "You scared me. I was just getting ready to head back up to the house." She pushed herself off the floor.

"I'm sorry. I didn't mean to frighten you. I stopped at the house first." Drew bent down and ran his hand through Phillip's coat. "Hey, Phillip."

He stood and stepped closer to Janie, feeling a little woozy when he caught the sweet, flowery scent of her perfume. "Are you ready to head out?"

Janie nodded. "I dropped Riley off at Buser's General earlier, so I didn't have time to grab a cup of coffee. I've got a fresh pot up at the house, if you're interested," she suggested, breezing toward the door.

"That sounds good to me." Drew turned toward the horses. "Looks like they're settling in nicely."

"Yes, they are. They were a little riled up when Mr. Harp first dropped them off, but they seem to be content. Mark will be stopping by soon to feed them and get them out into the pasture."

As they stepped out into the bright sunlight, a red-tailed hawk cried out in the sky and Drew looked up. "Mark's a hard worker."

"He really is. Oh, that reminds me. Mark has two friends he's bringing by next week—both are looking for jobs. He said they work just as hard as he does. I thought it would be good to start lining up some interviews since August fifteenth will be here before we know it."

Drew liked that Janie was taking the initiative. The outdoor center was her business too, so he wanted her to be as involved as her schedule would allow. Once school started, the weekly day-camp activities would come to an end until next summer. Drew and Janie had both agreed they'd start booking overnight stays for out-of-town guests participating in activities at the sporting facility. The crew working on the cabin renovations would be finished by the fifteenth. "That's smart thinking, Janie." He nudged her arm. "See, you do have a good business head on your shoulders."

Following a leisurely cup of coffee and some brainstorming on their business plan, the drive to Lexington's Heritage was going much too fast. Drew wasn't sure if it was the caffeine or just being away from the camp and all of the responsibilities, but Janie chatted up a storm—sharing stories of Riley's first steps and how one year, two days before Christmas, she'd snuck out of bed and unwrapped all of the gifts under the tree. During all the reminiscing she never mentioned her ex-husband. Since Janie had returned to town there'd been times she seemed like a frightened, timid animal. Like the ones he'd seen at the pet rescues with sadness in their eyes. But today, as she spoke about her daughter, Janie glowed. Drew hit the turn signal when he arrived at the exit for Shane's shop.

"We're here already?" Janie gazed out the window.

"Yep, it's right up ahead."

Moments later, Drew steered the truck onto a dirt road, encompassing the vehicle in a cloud of dust. Drew hit the button to close the windows.

The red-and-yellow open-for-business sign hung across the double-framed front door of the structure that resembled a barn. Drew parked and unlatched his seat belt, quickly exited and rounded the vehicle to Janie's door. Opening it, he extended his hand to help her out.

For the second time today he enjoyed the fragrance trailing behind her.

"Thank you." Janie's cheeks tinted a shade of pink.

Drew took notice of the number of cars in the lot. He hoped Shane could help him today. When Drew had called earlier in the week, Shane told him an appointment wasn't necessary and to just come up when he could. Maybe Saturday wasn't the best day.

Inside the shop, Shane immediately spotted the twosome, waved and crossed the room. He extended his hand. "Drew, it's great to see you." With a firm handshake and a fit, muscular build, Shane didn't look anything like a man approaching his seventies.

"It's good to see you, too." He turned to Janie. "This is Janie Edmiston. We grew up together. She and her daughter have recently returned to Whispering Slopes."

Shane reached for Janie's hand. "It's a pleasure."

Over the next twenty minutes, Shane gave Drew and Janie his undivided attention. Strolling through the store, he pointed out the various saddles while Drew explained their needs.

"You might be sitting on a gold mine with this new business venture, Drew. You'll be the only business in the surrounding area to offer outdoor activities through the winter months, outside of downhill skiing. It's a brilliant idea, young man."

Drew noticed Janie looking at him and smiling. "Well, time will tell, I suppose."

"I agree, Shane. I think Drew's dream is going to be quite successful. I'm just thankful to be a part of it."

"Well, I'll definitely be one of your first patrons. My two grandsons would love it. Now, let's pick out your gear so you're all set for the group on Monday."

An hour later, Drew and Janie were back on the road. The trip had been successful. Loaded in the back of the trunk were twelve saddles. They were a big expense, but Shane gave them a 20 percent discount to show his support for the new business.

Janie remained quiet while Drew snuck glances in her direction. "Are you hungry?"

Gazing out the window she turned with a smile. "Actually, I'm starving. Coffee for breakfast doesn't really cut it."

Since the temperature was cooler than normal summer weather, Drew had an idea. "What time do you need to pick up Riley?"

"Mrs. Buser said she could use Riley's help until the store closes at six o'clock."

Glancing at the clock on the dashboard, Drew hit his turn signal when he came upon the sign for Valley Market. "When was the last time you went on a picnic?" Judging from her slow response time, Drew figured it had been a while.

Janie placed her index finger to her lip. "Actually, I don't even remember."

"Well, what do you say we refresh that memory? I know the perfect spot. Ruth, at Valley Market, makes the best fried chicken in the Shenandoah Valley." Drew licked his lips. "I can taste it now."

Janie laughed. "That good, huh?"

"Trust me. What do you say?" Drew hoped for a yes. He found himself feeling excited at the prospect of a picnic for two.

"Okay, you've convinced me. I've never been able to resist fried chicken." Janie smiled.

Drew had loved to go on picnics with his family. He

recalled the first time he and his wife took Heidi picnicking. His daughter ran through the open meadow until she was breathless. Finally flopping down on the blanket between her parents, she looked up at Drew and told him she wanted to do this every Sunday after church. And so the tradition began. Funny, not long ago, recalling those special moments caused too much pain for him. But now, in Janie's presence, thinking about his family seemed cathartic. "Going on a picnic used to be my daughter's favorite thing to do." Drew pulled the truck up in front of the market and turned off the engine.

Janie reached over the console and placed her hand on Drew's forearm. "Thank you for sharing that with me."

He gazed out the windshield "Maybe next time we can bring Riley along." Was that what he wanted? More time with Janie and her daughter, outside of work?

"I think she would love that, Drew."

As they exited the truck and headed inside to pick up their meal, Drew's thoughts turned to their pastor's recent sermon. It had been as though he was speaking directly to Drew when he spoke about not dwelling in the past. He held the door for Janie. Could he let go of the former things and make Janie and Riley part of his future?

Janie kept a close eye on Drew as he shook out a red-and-white-checkered tablecloth, provided by Ruth. He spread it over the only cedar picnic table in the grassy clearing. Across the field, a tire swing hung from an enormous weeping willow branch. It was as though someone had created their own special sanctuary.

Drew removed several plastic containers from the brown paper bag and placed them on the table. Next in line came the paper plates, napkins, plastic forks and finally two cups, which he filled with sweet tea from the Thermos.

"You thought of everything." Janie took a sip of her drink.

"I can't take all of the credit. In the past, I've always gotten the picnic fixings from Ruth, so she remembered." Drew rolled down the top of the bag. "We'll keep the dessert a secret."

"What is it?" Janie pleaded, crinkling her nose. "I want to see."

He shook his head. "Nope. First you have to eat all of your meal." Drew smiled.

Janie's eyes popped as she inhaled the delicious aromas. Her stomach grumbled in response. "There's enough food here to feed the entire town. And that chicken looks amazing." Her eyes went to the buttery mashed potatoes with ground pepper and chives sprinkled on top.

"Those were always your favorite. I ordered extra butter." Drew winked.

Janie was touched that he remembered. While she was growing up, her mother made the best mashed potatoes. A recipe passed down from her grandmother. They were always smooth. During Janie's marriage she made several failed attempts at re-creating the recipe. Although Riley always enjoyed them and bragged how good they were, Randy had criticized them saying he wouldn't feed them to a dog. Janie's body shivered thinking about his icy words. Trying to stay in the moment, she forced them from her mind. "Thank you for remembering."

For the next forty minutes, the couple enjoyed their meal while exchanging various ideas for the sports center. It had been a long time since Janie shared a meal with a man who praised her ideas rather than making her feel inferior. Drew was a good friend—a good man.

"You were right, Drew. This is the best chicken ever." Janie licked her fingers, enjoying the tantalizing juices. "It's so crispy, but not dried out. I could never get mine to come out this way." Randy always reminded her of that. "How does Ruth do it?"

Drew laughed, shrugging his shoulders. "It's one of the many secrets in the Shenandoah Valley. It's a recipe Ruth says will never be revealed. Trust me—many townspeople have tried to replicate it, but so far, no one has cracked the code."

After their lunch, Drew cleared the table and stowed everything in his truck. He returned with a blanket and suggested they take a seat near the weeping willow tree.

Janie's stomach was ready to burst. She leaned back with her elbows resting on the fabric and her legs extended out in front her. She tipped her face to the warmth of the sun. Listening to the hum of the cicadas and the Shenandoah River's rushing water in the distance, she felt more relaxed than she'd been in years. She watched Drew, who was taking in the surroundings. It was obvious that this spot meant a lot to him. "I noticed there's only one picnic table—" she pointed to the tree "—and the swing. Is this where you came with your family?" As soon as she asked, she was filled with regret. Perhaps it was too painful to talk about it. "I'm

sorry. You don't have to answer that question. It's just…
this is such a beautiful area. You seem at peace here."

Drew hesitated before answering. Janie considered
him as he looked up at the sky.

"Yes, this is where my family and I came every
Sunday—if the weather permitted."

Silence lingered before he spoke again. "This is the
first time I've come back." He locked his eyes on Janie.
"I wanted it to be with you." His voice a whisper.

Janie wasn't prepared for this.

"I'm sorry. Is that too much? You're right, though. I
am at peace here, but I think a lot of it is because I'm
here with you."

The young Janie would have been thrilled to hear
Drew speak those words, but that girl no longer existed.
Grown-up Janie had too much baggage. Drew deserved
someone who was capable of loving and trusting him.
Not someone who believed they were no longer marriage material. If he knew the truth, he would have never
brought her to this special place.

"Hey, Janie?" He placed his hand underneath her
chin, tilting her face toward his. "Where did you go
just now?"

Janie's mind swirled with excuses. Admitting the
truth could put a strain on their business relationship,
as well as their friendship. Both things she cherished.
She didn't want Drew's pity. She didn't want him to ask
why she didn't leave the first time her ex-husband had
raised his hand to her. How could she continue to work
with someone who knew the truth about her past? She
couldn't. So she chose to remain silent.

Chapter Fourteen

As Drew poured his first cup of coffee on Monday morning, his cell phone chirped. With his hot beverage in hand, he walked to the kitchen table and picked up his device. "Hey, Skip. What's up?" He glanced out the window, where the sun was barely peeking over the tree-lined property.

"We've got a little problem." Skip's breath sounded quick.

"Did you just run a marathon or something? I haven't even had caffeine yet." Drew braced himself for the problem, hoping it was one with an easy solution.

"I'm at the farm. I gave Janie a call last night to give her a heads-up that I'd be stopping by this morning. I had forgotten my toolbox in the barn last week," he added. "I'm starting a job today at the Tuckers' place. When I got to Janie's, I noticed a portion of the fencing on the east side of the barn was compromised. Mark had let the horses out before I realized there was an issue with the fence."

Drew breathed a sigh of relief. "That's no big deal. I can take care of it before our ride this morning."

"Well, that's not the problem. Two of the horses have gotten loose. I know Janie has that group going out, but those animals are nowhere to be found." The tension in Skip's voice alarmed Drew.

Oh boy. Drew ran his hand through his hair. A sick feeling rolled through his stomach. Of all days, Janie had already been anxious about the ride today. She had learned that one of the kids who had signed up was the son of Tim O'Reilly, a well-known travel-magazine writer who planned on spending the morning riding with his child. Janie had hoped if the boy had a good time, the writer might do a piece on the camp. The last thing Drew wanted was for her to get wind of the escaped horses. "I'll be right over. If you see Janie, don't mention this."

"You got it," Skip quickly assured him.

Drew ended the call, squared his shoulders and headed outside.

Thirty minutes later Drew's truck hugged the winding mountain road in search of the horses. Before leaving the house, he'd called several business owners around town to ask them to keep an eye out for the animals. He also suggested they mention the loose animals to their patrons. The more people who knew, the better the chances were the horses would be found unharmed. He reached for the water bottle in the cup holder and took a long pull.

After circling the downtown area twice, Drew sucked in a breath, realizing he'd have to tell Janie about the horses. He turned the wheel in the direction of the farm.

Within seconds of his arrival, Drew realized Janie already knew. Her front yard was buzzing with activity as townspeople huddled together, each pointing in different directions. When he spied Janie in the crowd, her expression was solemn.

He parked the vehicle, removed his key and swung his feet to the ground. As he approached the group he heard chatter about the police and fire department.

"Drew!" Janie called out when she saw him approaching. "Two of the horses have gone missing."

Drew slid his hands into the front pockets of his jeans. "Yeah, Skip called me this morning. I've been driving around looking, but I didn't see them."

"Should I call the sheriff's department?" Janie powered on her phone.

A collision between a horse and an automobile could have a bad ending. "Yes. Give them a description of the animals." Drew turned to Mark before glancing at his watch. "What time did you feed them this morning?"

"It was around six o'clock," the young man answered.

"They could be anywhere by now," Janie cried out, scrolling for the number on her phone.

Minutes later, Skip rode up on one of the other horses. "I'm going to take a ride over toward the Millers' place. They've got that large clearing on their property. In the past, wandering animals have headed over there."

Drew agreed. He'd always heard the animals preferred an open area over the woods. "I'll ride over with you. Let me run down to the barn."

"I've got one of the horses saddled and ready to go," Skip answered.

Skip was always one step ahead of the game, which Drew appreciated. "I'll meet you at the gate," Drew called out as he jogged through the field toward the stalls.

Ten minutes into the ride, Drew and Skip rode in silence, except for the clomping of hooves traipsing along the trampled grassy path. Despite a brilliant sun overhead, the low humidity made the air comfortable for the middle of July. It was a perfect day for Janie's first official outing—if they could only find these animals.

Skip terminated the silence. "So this trail ride today is important to Janie?"

A successful ride today could help draw more business to the camp, and a writeup in a national magazine could boost business at the outdoor sporting center. "Actually, it's important for both of us." Drew explained about the special guest and how the event could lead to more business in the future.

"Well, we better speed up our search then." Skip pushed his hips forward in the saddle.

Drew applied a little more pressure to the horse's side with his legs to stay in pace with his friend.

Crowning the hill overlooking the Millers' property, Drew's shoulders relaxed. "You were right, Skip. There they are." Drew pointed to the two animals grazing as though they were exactly where they belonged. "I'll give the sheriff's office a quick call to let them know all is well. Let's hurry and get the horses home. The guests will be arriving soon."

When they got back to the barn, Drew secured the two horses in their stalls. "Thanks for everything, Skip. Sorry if I made you late for your job."

"No worries. I phoned the Tuckers earlier. They'd heard about the search, so they knew I'd be delayed."

Drew laughed. "Of course—life in a small town, right?"

A smile touched the corners of Skip's mouth. "See you later, bud. I hope today goes well."

The sound of whistling brought Drew outside the barn and under the warmth of the sun. His heart melted when he spotted Riley skipping through the field. With her hair in two high ponytails, she advanced in his direction. She glanced up and an enormous smile spread across her face before she took off running toward him.

"Mr. Drew! Mr. Drew! Did you find the horses?" she yelled as she neared the barn. Panting, she stopped at his feet. "Are they okay?"

He ran his hand over the top of her head. "Yes, they are safe inside, munchkin."

"Phew. I thought the day was going to be ruined." Riley looked up at Drew and her eyes widened.

"No, everything will be fine. Where's your mother?"

With two fingers, Riley stretched a bright pink piece of bubblegum from her mouth. "She's up at the house… worrying. She's always worried about something."

"Maybe we better head on up and give her the good news so she'll stop fretting. I tried to call her, but it went straight to voicemail." Truth be told, Drew had been a little concerned, as well. When Skip first called him this morning, he'd envisioned a much different outcome.

As the two strolled up the hill, Riley grabbed Drew's hand. His eyes skimmed down and he smiled. Despite the rough start, today was going to be a wonderful day.

Janie sat at the kitchen table and stared at the laptop screen before slamming it closed. She pushed the computer as far as her arms could stretch with hopes it would make the email from her ex go away, as well. It didn't. Following her attorney's advice, she hadn't responded to Randy's numerous emails. It was obvious he had no intention of going through the proper legal avenues to see Riley, so all she could do was hit the delete key. How could she move on with her life if he constantly tried to make contact with her?

A gentle summer breeze blew the yellow, sheer curtains hanging over the window, creating a chill through her body. She pulled down the sleeves on her jacket, covering her hands. With the horses missing and now these emails, Janie's day hadn't started well. She tried to stay positive, but Randy's belittling words kept repeating in her head, filling her with self-doubt.

"Mommy!"

Janie's mood lifted at the sweet sound of her daughter's voice. Turning, her chest was light at the sight of Drew entering the kitchen holding Riley's hand. The look he gave Janie stirred something inside her. That something had to be nipped in the bud if they planned to work together.

"Mr. Drew and Mr. Skip found the horses!" She ran toward her mother with a look of concern. "You don't have to worry anymore. Everything is going to be okay—Mr. Drew said so."

Drew stepped toward Janie and placed his hand on her shoulder. "Are you okay? I tried to call."

His easy smile warmed her. "Oh, I just took the phone off the charger. I'm fine now." Drew didn't appear convinced. At least one problem had been solved, but the bigger one still remained in her email account. "Thank you so much for tracking down the horses. I wasn't sure how I'd be able to handle the tour today being two horses short."

Janie rose from her chair. "Let me get you some coffee."

"That sounds perfect." Drew walked toward the

counter. "Actually, you can thank Skip for finding the animals. He was the one who knew to look at the Millers' place."

She passed the cup to Drew. "Well, I'm just glad they're back." She headed to the table and took a seat.

"Mommy, what time are the people coming for the ride?" Riley did a half spin before jerking to a halt and smiling at Drew.

"Are you getting a little anxious, munchkin?" Drew sipped his brew.

Riley's face scrunched up. "Just a little—plus, I'm bored."

Janie planned to take care of some paperwork before the guests arrived, but Randy had thrown her off track. Glancing at the time, she turned her attention to Riley. "They should be here in about forty-five minutes. Why don't you go down to the barn and see if Mark and Laura Marie need any help."

"Cool!" Riley dashed out the back door with Frankie on her heels.

Drew raised a brow. "I don't think I've ever had that much energy."

Janie couldn't get Randy out of her mind. Even divorced, he still controlled her.

"Janie? What's up?" Drew slid into the chair next to hers. "I know you. Something is bothering you."

Yes. He did know her. She found comfort in thinking about the number of years they'd been friends, but she wasn't sure if she wanted to burden him with her personal issues. But wasn't that what friends were for? To listen to each other's problems and offer support. But she feared sharing too much could change the way Drew felt about her, so she'd only share a little. "It's

Randy...my ex." Uneasiness spread through her gut. How could she stop giving him the power?

"What about him?" Drew's eyes narrowed.

She swallowed hard, but her throat continued to tighten. "He wants to see Riley."

Drew leaned in closer. "Has he called you?"

"No. He's sending emails. My attorney told me to tell him to contact his attorney if he wants to file for custody or visitation. I did and I haven't opened any of his emails since." Janie splayed her hands across the table. "But he keeps writing."

"Maybe if you continue ignoring him, he'll get the hint and contact his lawyer. The man wants to see his child, but he needs to follow the law."

Janie nodded. "I agree, but ignoring him won't make him stop. I know him too well. He's going to do things his way. He always has."

Drew rubbed the back of his neck. "Do you think he'd come here to see Riley?"

Janie's stomach squeezed. "He's been here already."

Drew's back straightened. "When? At the farm?"

She explained how she thought she'd seen him at the fair, but it was confirmed when Randy started sending her emails. Janie watched Drew as his shoulders stiffened and his brow furrowed. "What is it, Drew?"

He mauled his face with his right hand. "The other day, when I was waiting for you here, after you got the keys to the house, a car came down the driveway. It stopped suddenly and then turned around."

Janie picked up her glass of water to stop the trembling in her hands. "Why didn't you tell me? Could you see who was behind the wheel?"

"No, the sun was reflecting off of the car and the

windows were tinted. I couldn't really see inside. Honestly, at the time, I didn't think too much of it. I assumed someone made a wrong turn off the main road," he explained.

"What kind of car was it?" Janie prepared herself for the answer she didn't want to hear.

"It was a dark, older sedan." He shook his head. "I couldn't tell the exact make or model."

Janie released a sigh of relief. "Randy drives a white SUV." Her worries mounted again when she realized he could have been driving a rental car.

Drew reached for her hand. "Try not to worry. He's probably back in Maryland." He hesitated before speaking again. "I wonder if any of his unopened emails would give you answers as to whether or not he's in Maryland or here."

Janie didn't see any harm in reading through the emails. For the safety of her daughter, wouldn't it be wise to read the messages? She reached across the table and opened the laptop. After logging into her account, she retrieved the previously deleted messages before turning the machine toward Drew. "Here, you read them. I want to make sure Riley is safe, but I don't want to hear anything Randy has to say."

"Are you sure? There might be things he's said that you rather I didn't know." Drew shifted in his chair.

Janie shook her head. "I'm done keeping secrets. Riley's safety is all that matters."

Drew slid the computer closer, and his eyes widened.

"What is it?" Her stomach grew queasy.

"He sure has sent a lot of emails." Drew continued to hit the down arrow key.

"I know. I told you. He doesn't like to be ignored."

Janie crossed her arms and leaned back into the chair. "Does he say anything about contacting his attorney?" She picked up her coffee cup. Even though it was cold, she clutched it between her hands.

Drew tapped on the keyboard. "Wait…he wants to see Riley without getting any lawyers involved. He says he's only looking out for your best interest because he knows you don't have the money for legal fees."

Janie shook her head and forced a fake laugh. The man had never cared about what was best for her. "What about being here in Whispering Slopes?"

"I don't see anything. Most of the emails seem to be duplicates." He pushed the computer off to the side. "So…what do you want to do about this?"

"Nothing now. Today is a big day. I want to head down to the stables and get the horses ready for our guests. Remember, we've got a famous writer coming along. We want to do everything we can to make sure he and his son have a wonderful time."

Drew rose from his chair and smiled. "That sounds like a good plan to me."

What more could she do? Then it dawned on her. If she allowed herself to continue to worry about this, Randy would still have all of the power. He would still be controlling her. Something he'd done for ten years because she allowed it. No more. She had a new business. A new life. She wasn't the old, damaged Janie any longer. She'd just ignore his emails and hopefully Randy would go away.

Chapter Fifteen

Riding along the winding mountain trail, Drew couldn't have been prouder of Janie. As a young girl, several years of riding lessons had made her more at ease on a horse than on a bicycle. Leading the group of nine children and three adults with an air of confidence he hadn't seen since she won the Shenandoah National Spelling Bee when they were in the ninth grade.

He listened as she discussed in detail specific flowers and trees native to the Shenandoah Valley. The children were full of questions about the wildlife and the Shenandoah River, which she answered in depth. Nothing went unanswered. It was obvious that Janie was in her element and she'd done her homework. Judging by the expression on Mr. O'Reilly's face, Janie had impressed him, as well. Drew hoped that the events from today would end up as a cover story for his magazine.

Janie tightened the reins on her horse and turned around to face the group. "Are you all ready to stop for some lunch?"

The children cheered a resounding yes as Janie continued to lead everyone down the path. Excited chatter filled the forest.

Mr. O'Reilly's horse rode up beside Drew and the man leaned in. "She sure knows her stuff, and she's great with the kids, isn't she?" he commented as the two lagged behind the group.

Drew could hardly take his eyes off Janie. It was obvious Mr. O'Reilly was intrigued, so the timing couldn't be better. "She'd make a great lead cover story. Don't you think?" Drew hadn't planned on being so forward, but Janie's confident attitude seemed to be rubbing off on him.

The man cleared his throat. "Actually no, I don't think she would."

Drew's shoulders slumped. How could he have misread Mr. O'Reilly? He'd seemed so captivated by Janie's knowledge. "I don't understand, sir." The smile he'd been wearing since the start of the ride slid from his face.

"I'm sorry, son. I meant to say I think you both—this place—would make a spectacular story. In an age where everyone is so connected to their electronic devices and not getting outside to appreciate nature, I think what you're doing here for the children is a wonderful thing. You should be proud."

Thank You, God. This was exactly what he'd prayed for last night. He wanted this so bad, not only for him, but for Janie. Since she'd returned to town, Drew had been fighting their connection, but he now knew it was a losing battle. He was in love with her. But did she feel the same way? "Mr. O'Reilly?"

"Please, call me Tim."

Drew nodded. "Tim it is. Could you not mention the

article to Janie today? I'd like to tell her myself." He couldn't wait to share the news. Just the two of them, over dinner in a nice restaurant. Or maybe he could cook dinner for her. She'd always loved spaghetti and meatballs. That just happened to be his specialty.

"Of course, son." Tim nodded as though he was aware of the feelings Drew had for Janie. "Mum's the word today, but I'll give you a call in a day or two to arrange a time to come back for the interview. I'll be bringing a photographer. We'll take a lot of photographs for the camp and your new business venture, as well. I want to get the word out about what you're doing."

Drew's head whirled like a windmill in a storm. "You're going to be doing the interview?"

"Of course. I want to take the credit for discovering this gem." He hesitated for a moment. "Really my son found you, but we'll keep that between ourselves." He winked. "Let's go eat. I'm starving." Mr. O'Reilly kicked his boots into the side of the horse and took off to catch up with the others.

Drew trailed behind, trying to absorb the conversation. He couldn't wait to see the look on Janie's face when he shared the big news. A part of him wanted to tell her now, since he felt like he could burst, but this was their news to share together—privately.

When everyone climbed off their horses at the large clearing surrounded by towering pines, Drew was relieved to see Mark and Laura Marie had arrived with the food. Six picnic tables filled the area, each covered with a tablecloth and a brown-bag lunch.

"Come sit with us, Mr. Drew!" Riley called from the table where she sat with Janie, Tim and his son.

After climbing down from his horse, Drew tethered

the reins to a nearby tree. As he headed toward the group, the sounds of children laughing and chattering echoed through the forest. Not long ago, he would have escaped to the safety of his isolated cabin. No more. He thought of Heidi and how much she would have loved an outing like this. Once at the table, pushing the sadness away, he slid onto the bench and snatched a bag. "What's for lunch?" He peeked into the bag, trying to appear as though he was being sneaky.

Riley giggled. "It's ham and cheese on rye with Mrs. Buser's homemade potato chips. They're really good." She grabbed one for herself.

Drew turned to Janie. "The woman makes homemade chips? Is there anything she can't do? And where in the world does she find the time?"

Janie nodded. "I know. She's got endless energy. I don't know how she does it. She's always busy."

Riley sat up straight. "Mrs. Buser says she's not busy. She calls it being fruitful." Riley reached for her bag and jumped up from the table. She motioned to Tim's son. "Let's go over and sit with Mark and Laura Marie."

Drew had been guilty of trying to stay as busy as possible. After the accident, he did everything he could to keep his mind occupied so he wouldn't have to think about his family. But now, his life had changed. He had a reason to get out of bed in the morning. There were people who depended on him. He was helping Janie and Riley build a better life and now, looking around at the children's smiling faces, he knew he was making a difference in their lives, too.

"I think I'm going to walk around a little bit and take in some more of the scenic view." Tim pushed away from the table, leaving Drew and Janie alone.

Drew picked at the napkin on the table, trying to get up the nerve to ask Janie out so he could share the exciting news. "You were really incredible out there today." He glanced up at Janie.

Her brow arched. "What do you mean?" She took a bite of her sandwich.

"On the trail—with the children. It all seemed to come so natural for you."

Janie blushed. "We were just riding."

Drew shook his head. "No, it was more than that. You captivated the kids with your knowledge of the landscape and wildlife. Trust me. I know how difficult it can be to keep a child's attention." He reached across the table and took her hand. "You should be proud of yourself, Janie. Take a second and think about what you've accomplished." He squeezed her hand and smiled. "And this is only the beginning."

She pulled away from his touch. "Thank you, Drew. That really means a lot."

Above, a lone hawk cried out while Drew gathered his thoughts. "Are you busy on Friday night?"

"I don't think I have anything planned. What's up?" Janie asked.

"Would you like to have dinner with me?" When her shoulders appeared to stiffen Drew realized he needed to rephrase his question or he might be shot down. "There're some things I wanted to discuss with you about the opening of the center."

Her body seemed to relax. "Oh, sure." She paused. "I guess we could do that."

"I thought I could cook your favorite dish, spaghetti and meatballs." Once again, she appeared tense. "Or we can go out…something casual. Pizza maybe?"

"That sounds good to me."

"Great. I'll come by your house around seven o'clock." Drew relaxed. He'd taken the first step.

Janie rose from the table. "That sounds good." Grabbing her brown bag, she gathered her trash before turning to him. "I'm going to check on the children."

Drew nodded and watched as she scurried toward the trash can. After dumping her garbage, she pulled on the sleeves of her sweatshirt and headed toward the other tables.

Drew picked up the last bite of his sandwich and paused. He and Janie were going to be featured in a national magazine. Unbelievable.

His mind started to go into overdrive. They would have to hire more staff. If their business increased even the slightest from the article, they wouldn't be able to handle the volume. They'd probably need more horses and maybe a wider variety of animals.

After losing his family, he'd thought his future would never seem bright again. Where there is light, there can be no darkness. He believed that now. God had brought light back into his world in His own special timing. Drew was ready to start living his life again. But what about Janie? Was she ready to move on and begin a new life with him? He could only hope and pray her answer would be yes.

Janie stood in front of the full-length mirror hanging from her bedroom door on Friday evening. Thankfully, the day had been so busy she hadn't had much time to think about her plans for tonight. Unfortunately, she hadn't thought about what she'd wear, either, but she was relieved she'd opted for dinner out rather than

Drew cooking for her in his cozy cabin. She wasn't sure she was ready for a man to cook a meal for her, even if it was Drew.

"How many times are you going to change your clothes, Mommy?" Riley sat perched on Janie's maple sleigh bed, cuddling with Frankie.

Janie turned around dressed in black skinny jeans and a long-sleeved cotton peasant blouse. Void of any jewelry, ballet flats completed her outfit. "What are you talking about?"

Riley scrunched her nose. "That's the third time you've tried on something different. I like that one the best." She smiled. "You look pretty."

Janie approached her daughter, giving her a kiss on the cheek. "Thank you, sweetie." She cupped Riley's chin, tilting her head up "I think you look pretty too, baby girl." She turned and walked back to the mirror. "Are you sure? Maybe I should try the dress on again," Janie said, heading toward the closet.

"No, that outfit is perfect for your date, Mommy."

Janie flinched. "It's not a date." Or was it? Drew had been acting a little odd when he invited her. He seemed almost giddy. Maybe he was just excited for the upcoming opening. Seeing a dream come true can cause a wave of emotions.

"If it's not a date, then what is it, Mommy?" Riley tilted her head.

The million-dollar question she'd been pondering since Monday. A part of her wanted this evening to be a date—the first of many with a man she'd always cared for. Something she'd dreamed about when they were younger. But then there was the flip side. Having a relationship meant taking risks, trusting that person wouldn't hurt you or try to control your life. It meant opening up about her past and revealing what was underneath her jacket. Janie wasn't sure she was capable of that. Correction—she couldn't do that. "Well, you know Mr. Drew and I are going into business together, right?"

Riley bounced up and down on the bed. "Yeah, the outdoor place. It's going to be so cool! There will probably be people coming from all over the world!"

Janie laughed. "Well, I'm not sure about that, but I appreciate your enthusiasm. That's what this dinner is about. With the grand opening only a couple of weeks away, we have a lot of things to discuss to ensure we're ready to open and that everything runs as smooth as possible. It's all business stuff."

"But shouldn't I go to dinner with you guys, since I'll be helping you run the place?" Riley questioned.

Janie smiled at her daughter's words. Riley had always been her mother's little helper. "The things we need to discuss probably won't be of much interest to you, sweetie. Besides, aren't you excited to have Mrs. Buser coming over to babysit?"

Riley smooshed her face into Frankie's coat then looked up. "Yeah, she said we could bake chocolate-chip cookies."

When the doorbell chimed, Riley sprang from the bed and ran to the front door. Janie's stomach tightened. She hoped it was Mrs. Buser and not Drew. Checking her hair in the mirror, she wasn't quite ready. Her nerves were getting the best of her. This nondate was beginning to feel more like the real thing. She sucked in a deep breath, exhaled and headed down the hall.

Once in the foyer, warmth spread into her heart when she spotted Drew kneeling as he talked to Riley. Janie noticed the look in her daughter's eyes as Drew gave her his undivided attention. Riley hung on to every word he said. When he presented her with a bouquet of daisies he had hidden behind his back, Janie thought Riley would burst with joy.

Riley accepted the flowers and raced toward Janie. "Look, Mommy! Mr. Drew gave me flowers!" She could hardly catch her breath. "No one has ever done that before!"

Drew crossed the floor and extended his other hand to Janie. "I didn't forget you."

As he handed her the flowers, their fingers brushed, igniting warmth in her face. "Thank you, Drew. I've always loved daisies."

"Me too, Mommy! They look like they're smiling. Don't they, Mr. Drew?"

The adults shared a laugh as the doorbell rang for the second time.

"That must be Mrs. Buser," Riley announced. "I'll let her in." The child headed back toward the door.

Janie stood face-to-face with Drew, connected like a magnet to metal. Neither one seemed to be able to look away.

"Good evening." Mrs. Buser stepped toward the couple.

Janie forced her focus away from Drew, but her heart continued to race.

"You look so pretty tonight," the elderly woman commented as she looked at Janie from head to foot.

Janie tilted her head to the ground. "Thank you." For some reason, she felt embarrassed that Drew had heard the compliment. She didn't want him to think she'd spent extra time on her appearance because she thought this outing was a date.

Drew placed his hand on Janie's arm. "Are you ready to head out?"

"Sure." She turned to Riley. "Be a good girl for Mrs. Buser." She gave her a quick peck on the cheek.

"I will, Mommy." She looked up with a smile. "Have fun on your date!" she exclaimed before running toward the kitchen. "I'll get the recipe for the cookies, Mrs. Buser."

The three adults stood in an awkward silence.

Drew looked at Janie and grinned. "Ready for your date?" He winked and placed his hand on her lower back, guiding her toward the front door.

Janie's nerves were jittery during the twenty-minute drive to the restaurant. Drew hadn't told her where they were going. He said it was a surprise. Her stomach was turning somersaults. How in the world would she be able to eat a meal? Right now, she couldn't even stomach a saltine cracker. When Drew had arrived at her house tonight, the attraction she'd always had for him intensified. Dressed in casual jeans and a crisp white-collared shirt, his captivating smile sent her pulse into overdrive. Could this really be a date?

Her anxieties settled a little when she stepped inside the restaurant. "I can't believe you brought me here," she said, smiling at Drew. While in high school Janie and Drew, along with a gang of other kids, always came to Vito's Pizzeria on Friday night. A quick scan of the room proved it had the same electrifying atmosphere she remembered. Packed with young people and adults, it was exactly as she remembered. And the same seat-yourself sign sat perched at the front door.

Drew took Janie's hand and the electricity intensified. "Let's take that corner booth over there." He pointed to the rustic table with an empty bottle covered with candle wax placed in the center.

"What happened to the red-checkered tablecloths?" Janie slipped into the seat.

"When Vito passed away about ten years ago, his son took over. He did a little remodeling, but tried to keep most of it the same."

Janie surveyed the wall lined with family photos displaying generations that had come before Vito's son. On the other side of the room a painted mural of an Italian café, owned by one of Vito's relatives, filled the entire wall. "Remember when we talked about one day going to that café?"

Drew gazed at the painting. "Yes, I do remember." He smiled.

The euphoric sense of nostalgia slipped away. "I guess life doesn't always turn out the way we dream it could be," Janie said.

The discussion stilled when a young waiter, carrying a pitcher of water and two glasses on a tray, approached the table. "Hi, Mr. Brenner."

Janie studied the young man. He bore a strong resemblance to the Vito she remembered growing up in Whispering Slopes.

"Janie, this is Vito's grandson Michael." Drew turned his attention back to the young waiter. "This is Janie Edmiston. She grew up here and recently moved home. She's Nick Capello's sister."

"Welcome home. We always love when Nick brings the family to the restaurant." Michael placed the glasses on the table and filled them to the top with icy water. "Do you want a few minutes to look at your options?"

Janie read the menu. It had expanded since she'd last eaten at the restaurant.

"What do you think, Janie? Should we have our usual?" Drew didn't touch his listing.

Their usual. It was exactly what she wanted. Turning to Drew, she closed the menu and nodded.

"We'll have the classic with everything on it," Drew told Michael. "And two iced teas."

"Extra cheese, please," Janie added.

"You got it." Michael collected the menus and headed off toward the kitchen.

Drew placed his hands on the table and folded his fingers together. "So, do you think we can eat the entire pizza like we did that one Friday night after our team won the state championship?"

Janie recalled that evening. Although it seemed like a lifetime ago, the memory remained vivid. Drew had thrown the winning touchdown and won their school the trophy. It was the first and only time the two had kissed. At the time, it was nothing more than the excitement of the moment. But for days after, she had dreamed about it. "I don't know—that's a pretty big pie. I might have to take some of mine home to Riley. Would that count?"

Drew laughed as Janie took a sip of her water, feeling more relaxed than she'd been all day. She looked around the restaurant before directing her eyes back on her date. Yes, that's what this was. Riley had been right. "This is nice. Thank you for bringing me here."

"One of the reasons I wanted to have dinner with you was to share some news."

Disappointment took hold. Maybe this wasn't a date

after all. Janie could only hope at least the news would be something good. "I hope it's positive."

Drew leaned in closer. "Earlier, you said that life doesn't always turn out the way we planned."

"Yeah, man plans, God laughs." Something her grandmother had always said.

"Well, that's about ready to change, Janie. Things have gone as planned—actually better than we had hoped. I've been dying to tell you, but I wanted to share the news in private."

It was true. She was rarely alone with Drew. Between Riley, the children visiting the camp and the staff, there was no time for any in-depth conversation. Even when they were both working in their shared office space, they were so swamped with paperwork. There was little time to really talk. At first she was happy about that, but the more time they spent together, the more she'd started to crave moments like this—just the two of them. She'd tried to fight the feeling, but lately her attraction to Drew was growing stronger. Janie leaned back, pushing her back against the chair. "What's the news?"

When Drew's lips parted into a smile that crossed his entire face, Janie couldn't wait one more second. "Tell me!" she said in a tone that caused the group of kids at a nearby table to turn.

Drew laughed and reached for her hands. "Tim wants to do a feature article for his magazine on the camp and the upcoming opening of the outdoor center."

Janie squealed and the kids looked over for a second time, laughing. She pulled a hand away from Drew's grasp and covered her mouth, shaking her head. Placing her hand back between his fingers, she latched on to his gaze. "I can't believe this, Drew. Are you sure?"

"I'm positive. You really impressed him, Janie. The trail ride on Monday sealed the deal." He squeezed her hand. "You impressed me, too. You're a strong and capable woman. Don't ever forget that."

As Michael approached with the pizza, Janie remained energized by the news. Never in her wildest dreams would she have imagined her life could take such a drastic turn. Drew's words touched her deep inside her heart. She'd never thought of herself as strong, much less capable. Well, maybe before she met Randy, but he'd made sure he stole every ounce of her self-confidence during their marriage. Sitting here with Drew, celebrating the news of something they'd accomplished together, she felt more like a couple than she ever had during her ten years with Randy. When she looked into Drew's eyes, an old flame, one she thought had been extinguished for years, suddenly ignited. She sat with her childhood friend, savoring the moment. Could she let go of the past and put her trust into another man?

Chapter Sixteen

"I knew we could do it," Drew fell back against the booth, holding his distended belly. He'd enjoyed every second of the past two hours. They'd nibbled on their pizza as they discussed plans for the outdoor center and they'd also reminisced about their childhood. The crowd had thinned, but the soft Italian music still drifted through the restaurant. Drew could stay right here for a lifetime. But did Janie feel the same?

"I think I got a second wind after the third piece." Janie laughed, holding her stomach and looking down. "I'm not sure how long my zipper is going to hold, though."

Michael approached the booth and cleared the empty pizza pan. "Wow! I'm not sure I've ever seen two people eat the entire combo alone. Usually it will feed an entire family." He removed their plates.

Drew looked up at the young man. "Are you trying to blow your tip?" He laughed.

"I'm just messing with you guys." He placed the tray of dirty dishes on a nearby table and pulled out his pad and pencil. "Can I offer you some dessert? We've got a terrific tiramisu."

Janie looked adorable as she let out a painful groan. "I couldn't eat another bite of anything, Michael. I think we're good for the next week."

Sliding his pad back into his apron pocket, he nodded. "Okay, how about a nice strawberry gelato to cleanse your palate?"

Drew raised a brow to Janie. "What do you think?"

"Actually, that sounds perfect, Michael." Janie played with a loose strand of hair.

"One gelato, two spoons," Drew ordered. "I think that's a safe choice."

"Honestly, I don't typically eat this much. I guess the exciting news worked up my appetite," Janie confessed.

"Well, you might need to go up another pant size because there is more excitement." Drew's telephone conversation with Tim on Thursday morning had set things into motion. "The photographer for the magazine plans to come to the farm on Monday."

"Oh my! Are you kidding, Drew?"

Seeing Janie this excited made him happier than he could remember. "It's true. When I told Tim you had booked another trail ride with a group of eight children, he thought it would be the perfect time to get some candid photos, rather than have posed pictures. Don't worry, I can handle getting written permission from all of the parents, first."

Janie placed her hands to her blushing cheeks. "That makes sense, but I'll be so nervous."

"You have nothing to be nervous about. Just do what you did last Monday and the photos will be spectacular."

Her eyebrows drew together. "Will you come on the ride, too?"

After Tim had mentioned the photo shoot, Drew had

hoped Janie would want him to be included. "Of course I will. They plan to do some photos of the both of us together to advertise the sporting center."

Janie rubbed her hand along her forehead. "This is all happening so fast. It's hard to wrap my head around it."

Drew agreed. The camp and the center were both changing their lives, but it was more than that. Working at the camp with Janie had opened his eyes to a world he'd stepped away from following the accident. But after the past few weeks and especially after tonight, he understood what he wanted—a life with Janie and Riley.

Later, after the couple shared their gelato and Drew paid the bill, he'd suggested they take a stroll around town to walk off their heavy meal.

Outside, the full moon reflected off the nearby lake. Stars twinkled in the inky sky, proof of endless possibilities. "It's a beautiful evening. The temperature couldn't be more perfect." He reached for Janie's hand. "Let's take a walk around the boardwalk."

Janie gazed out over the water before turning her attention to Drew. "The lake is absolutely gorgeous." Her eyes sparkled in the evening light. "Thank you so much for bringing me here. This night has been perfect. I couldn't think of a better place for you to share the wonderful news about the magazine piece."

With one hand, Drew guided Janie toward the railing. He cupped her chin, turning her face toward his. Tilting her head upward, he closed the distance between them. When she followed his lead, her warm breath tickled his skin. He slowly leaned in and brushed his lips against hers. Sweet as summertime strawberries, he lost himself in the gentleness of her kiss. He ran his fingers through her cascading hair as their kiss deepened and his heart hammered against his chest. Pulling back, his eyes fixed on hers.

He paused for her reaction. Was this too much, too soon? Would kissing her jeopardize their business partnership? She responded with no words, but only a second kiss that left Drew hopeful for their future.

The group was twenty minutes into the trail ride and if Janie was nervous, she hid it well. She looked cool as a cucumber. Steve the photographer was a pro. He snapped candid shots discreetly. Was Janie even aware of his presence?

"Can we head down toward the river?" Steve asked. "I'd like to get a group photograph with the Shenandoah in the background."

When they arrived at the riverbank, Janie turned to Steve, shielding them from the sun filtering through the trees with her hand. "Would you like us to stay on our horses or stand as a group?"

Steve looked around. "Let's try both and see which one works best. Is that okay with you kids?"

The children all cheered. Earlier, when the parents dropped their kids off for the day, Drew had let the adults know about the photographer and had obtained signed permission for the outing. He wanted to make sure they were okay with the possibility of their child's picture turning up in a national magazine. None of the parents had any privacy concerns and the children were ecstatic.

As the day passed, Drew's face hurt from all of the smiling. Steve had finished with the camp photos and the children had gone with Mark and Laura Marie to get things ready for the cookout. Steve moved on to the shots with Drew and Janie to promote the sports center. Thankfully, the sign company had made a delivery late last week, so the new business partners were photographed standing in front of the towering sign that read Welcome to Rocky River Camp and Outdoor Adventures.

Janie was glowing. Drew had never seen her happier. A part of him hoped some of her happiness was due to the kiss they'd shared Friday night, but since neither had spoken about it, he wasn't sure. One thing he did know, he was looking forward to an encore performance. He planned to ask her out on a real date. No pretending it was to discuss the business. First he had to check Mrs. Buser's schedule to make sure she'd be available to watch Riley.

"I got some really great photographs to work with. Thank you both." Steve packed his camera equipment into a leather case. "You'll love the pictures with the two of you in front of the sign. I'm sure one of them will be used on the cover of the magazine."

Drew heard Janie gasp as she grabbed his arm. "We're going to be on the cover?" Her voice shook.

Steve smiled. "That's Tim's plan. He'd like to run the article as soon as possible. He wants to make sure you get exposure for your opening day."

Drew's mind whirled from the news. "Don't you have to schedule these stories months in advance?" He wasn't quite sure how the publishing industry worked.

"Typically, yes. Tim really believes in what you're doing here for the kids and the community, so he's bumping another cover story to a later date."

Janie squeezed Drew's arm. "This is all so amazing. I don't know how we can ever repay you and Tim."

"No need for that." Steve adjusted the camera-case

strap over his shoulder. "Our magazine is in the business of promoting the importance of outdoor life, especially for children. Your company is a great example. The next time I visit, I plan to leave my camera at home and bring my twin daughters along to spend the day."

Janie stepped forward, extending her hand. "You and your family are welcome anytime, Steve. Thank you for everything." She turned and guided her horse up the path.

Drew escorted Steve to his truck where he was told Tim would be in touch soon. Climbing on the horse, Drew headed back toward the activity building to get the grill fired up for a cookout. He paused and took in the moment. Things had changed so much in the weeks since Janie returned to Whispering Slopes. He was living once again. It was what his wife would have wanted. He gave thanks to God and made his way up the hill toward his future.

"Hey, munchkin." He halted the horse. "Where's your mother?" Drew approached Riley and the buzzing group of children playing horseshoes with Laura Marie.

"She's still down at the stables. She said she wanted to clean out the stalls a little and would be right up. We offered to help, but she said she was fine." Riley flung a horseshoe toward the stake.

Drew watched as the shoe landed close. "Nice shot, munchkin. You guys keep playing and I'll go down to check on your mother."

Minutes later, Drew's horse slowed outside the barn. Inside, he heard Janie humming a tune he couldn't quite recognize, but it was upbeat. She was as happy with the trail ride today as he had been.

He climbed off the animal and slowly entered the structure. "Hey, you—"

"Drew!" Janie's eyes bulged. "What are you doing here?" she shouted in a tone unlike her.

Something was different. He followed her gaze and spotted a jacket flung over a stall door. That was it. She wasn't wearing her outerwear.

"Please go!" she cried out, sucking in shaky breaths.

He turned his focus back to Janie. She was cowered on the hay-covered ground with her arms wrapped tightly against her chest and her head down.

"Please, Drew…just go." She rocked back and forth.

Straw crunched underneath his shoes as he moved closer. "Janie, what's wrong? Let me help you." He dropped to his knees. His breath caught in his throat when, for the first time, he saw her bare arms.

Why did I take off my jacket? Since Drew entered the stable, the question had replayed through Janie's mind over and over. Earlier, she'd gotten overheated cleaning the stalls. No one was supposed to be here. She was safe, so she hung the coat over the door of the first stall. She should have known better. The only secure place was behind the locked door in her bedroom. Why did he have to come?

Drew extended his hand. "Let me help you up."

Janie tried to cover her skin. "Please, I'm begging you…just leave me alone."

"What happened, Janie? You can tell me." He sat down beside her. "You can trust me. I'll always be here for you."

Her back stiffened. Trust. Something her husband had stolen from her, but Drew was different. He always had been. Unable to hold back any longer, more tears erupted. "I'm so ashamed. I didn't want you to find out." Knowing that her secret was exposed, she extended her arms out in front of her. "He burned me," she whispered. The shame still seared.

Drew lifted his hand as if to touch the scars, then dropped it to his side. "Your ex did this to you?"

She nodded and looked into Drew's eyes. He wiped away a tear running down his cheek.

"Oh, Janie. I'm so sorry." He opened his arms for her in invitation, and she went into his embrace.

The warmth of his touch provided strength. She sucked in a breath and exhaled. "I should have never married him. There were signs, early on, but I ignored them. I deserved this."

"Don't say that." He held her arms, gently caressing them. "No one deserves this."

"I should have walked away. The first time he hit me, I should have ended our relationship, but I stayed. How pathetic does that sound?" She rubbed her watery eyes, barely able to look at Drew. "He struck me on our second date."

Janie recalled that horrible night. Randy had been angry when he picked Janie up at her dormitory. He said he'd been arguing with his father. He didn't like the way his father treated his mother. Janie suggested perhaps his father should seek some help. Instead of agreeing, he'd backhanded her. He'd told her she needed to mind her own business.

She shuddered at the memory. "I thought I could change him. But the longer I stayed, the more he tore down my self-esteem. He told me no one would ever want me because I couldn't do anything right, not even care for our daughter. I tried to mold myself into the woman he wanted me to be, but it never was good enough."

Drew rocked her in his arms and stroked her hair. "You know that's not true, don't you? You're a wonderful mother."

She shook her head. "No, I second-guess every decision I make when it comes to Riley."

"Every parent does that, Janie. Trust me. Your daughter is one of the most well-adjusted children I've ever met. And as for you, I wish you could see yourself as others do. Just look at all that you've accomplished since you've moved home."

Janie wanted to believe that, but doubt always won. "I couldn't have done any of it without you. Just like Randy always said."

"That's not true, Janie. You need to forget the things Randy told you. What he said is not who you are. Not even close. He was only trying to control you. But he can't anymore…you're free of him."

A quick glance at her arms revealed the truth. It was branded into her skin. "I'll never be free from him. He made sure of that." Every time Randy came home late after a night of drinking, Janie would try to pretend to be asleep. That's when he would light his cigar and push it into her arm. The first couple of times, the pain felt unbearable, but eventually, she became numb. When she started believing she deserved it, she knew she had to break free from her marriage, not only for herself, but for Riley.

"You don't need to hide your scars any longer," Drew whispered. "Don't let the past define who you are today."

With those words, Janie found comfort in Drew's arms. *A time to keep, and a time to cast away.* She'd meditated on that verse during her divorce proceedings. Now she realized, she may have cast away her marriage, but she hadn't done the same with the wounds Randy had inflicted upon her.

Drew was right, not only had Randy been trying to control her throughout their marriage…he still was. No more. Her counselor in Maryland had told her she'd never be able to move on if she didn't let go of the shame and hurt. She'd recommended Janie have a conversation with Riley to delicately share why her parents' marriage ended. With all of the good happening in her life, Janie realized she needed to trust God with the new beginnings He was providing.

Janie stayed in Drew's arms, savoring the comfort he provided.

"Mommy. Are you in here?"

Janie jumped. Her pulse raced at the sound of Riley's voice as she entered the barn.

"Now's the time," Drew whispered into Janie's ear.

"Will you stay with me while I talk with her?" Janie wasn't sure she had the strength to do this alone. With Drew beside her, she felt more confident.

"Of course," he answered.

Janie cleared her throat and rose to her feet. "I'm over here, sweetie."

Riley moved toward her mother, but slowed when her eyes locked on to Janie's arms. "Are you hurt, Mommy? Did you fall or something?"

"No, I'm fine." She extended her hand. "Come, sit with me." Janie guided her daughter toward a stack of hay bales. Janie glanced in Drew's direction and he nodded.

She fought back the tears when Riley's fingers moved down her arms.

"Does it hurt?"

"No, sweetie. These are old scars that have healed." When Janie spoke those words for the first time, she was finally able to believe them.

"Is that why you always covered them?"

"Yes, but it was wrong of me. I shouldn't have been ashamed, but I was…for a long time."

Riley studied the scars before looking up at Janie. "Did Daddy do that to you?"

Janie's heart sank. As much as she'd tried to protect her daughter and not expose her to what was going on with her parents' marriage, she'd known. Swallowing hard, Janie struggled to speak. "Yes…he did."

Riley nuzzled her head against Janie's side. "I used to hear him yelling, but I pretended I didn't."

"Were you afraid?" The thought of her daughter being frightened in her own home broke her heart. Children should feel safe with their parents.

"Sometimes I was, but usually I was sad that Daddy made you cry so much."

Janie's heart broke for her daughter. She'd always assumed Riley wasn't aware of the abuse going on in the house. She'd been wrong. All along she'd wanted to protect Riley. But she hadn't. She'd made so many wrong decisions when it came to her marriage, particularly not to get out sooner. As she took Riley into her arms, Janie asked God for forgiveness. She also prayed that her poor judgment wouldn't negatively impact her daughter's life going forward.

Chapter Seventeen

"Are you sure you want to do this? I seem to recall you had a fear of heights." Taking his eyes off the road for a second, Drew stole a quick glance at Janie perched in his passenger seat. Adrenaline coursed through his veins. He had a hike scheduled with a group of children later this afternoon. But now, Mark and Laura Marie were covering the camp activities and Riley was helping Mrs. Buser at the store. The thought of spending early Wednesday afternoon together sounded perfect. With her hair swept up in a loose bun, dressed in khaki shorts and a short-sleeved T-shirt, Janie looked beautiful.

"Well, if we're going to offer rock climbing at our center, I think it's important that I learn a little about it." Janie took a sip of coffee from her insulated travel mug.

Drew admired her courage, but he and Janie had already hired two additional college students. "Remember, Mitch and Greg will be the guides. They'll be the ones taking our guests for the climbs. So you can keep your feet firmly on the ground," he joked.

She turned and peered out the window. "Actually,

I think it's time for me to start taking more risks. You know, step out of my comfort zone."

"I think you've made a good start." He placed his hand on her exposed arm.

Janie looked down. "Thanks. You know, at first I was angry when you caught me without my jacket, but it was time. Riley needed to know the truth, and I had to stop hiding from my past. I'm not sure I would have been able to tell her if you hadn't been there with me."

"I'm proud of you, Janie." Easing his foot off the accelerator as they approached the flashing lights at the railroad crossing, he turned to Janie. "You're the strongest person I know."

Janie half laughed. "You must not know many people." She shook her head.

"I'm serious. I don't know half of what you experienced during your marriage, but you were strong enough to get out."

"I should have left sooner." Her eyelashes fluttered as a tear ran down her face.

"Don't second-guess yourself. You've come too far."

The train released a whistle as it barreled down the tracks. The cars continued to pass in a blur and then they were gone. When the lights went out and the gate lifted, Drew pushed his foot on the gas, but his hand remained with Janie.

"You know, you've come pretty far yourself, Drew."

Drew considered her words. She and Riley had brought him back to life. He never imagined he'd ever consider a relationship again, but now, he couldn't get it out of his mind.

"What? You don't agree?" Janie removed her hand to pull down the sun visor.

"On the contrary, I completely agree with you. But you're the reason. If you hadn't moved back to Whispering Slopes, I would still be holed up in my cabin, missing out on life."

She shook her head. "I'm sure you would have moved on when you were ready. You were grieving the loss of your family."

"I had no reason to live. A part of me felt like I didn't deserve to be alive, since I believed the accident was my fault," Drew confessed.

Silence lingered inside the truck.

"We're quite a pair, aren't we?" Janie said.

Drew had avoided talking about their date the other night. He didn't want to put any pressure on Janie, but now seemed like a perfect opportunity. "I hope our kiss the other night during our walk didn't scare you. I just needed you to know how I feel."

"It's not the kiss that scares me, Drew."

"Then what is it?"

"It's…I'm just so messed up." She reached to cover her arms, but then dropped her hands into her lap. "I married someone who'd been abusive while we were dating. It wasn't like it all started after I said *I do*."

Drew wasn't qualified to analyze the decisions Janie had made in her past. He'd made his fair share of mistakes, so he listened.

"There's a part of me that wonders if I would have made the same choice if my upbringing had been any different. Losing my mother to drug addiction and then watching my father struggle after her death—I felt so alone. I wanted someone to love me." She could no longer hold back the tears.

Drew hit his turn signal and pulled into Morrison's

Gas and Go parking lot. He unbuckled his seat belt and moved closer, taking her into his arms. "Go ahead and let it out."

Moments later, when the cries subsided, Janie picked her purse up off the floor and pulled out a tissue. Rubbing her eyes, she turned to Drew. "I'm sorry."

He shook his head. "Don't be."

"Funny, after I went through the divorce, I had a couple therapy sessions and I never cried. Honestly, I didn't think about why I married Randy, knowing he was abusive. My therapist seemed to focus more on why I left rather than why I got involved with him in the first place." She blotted her eyes.

"I guess I make a pretty good therapist." He nudged her with his shoulder. "I'll send you my bill."

Janie laughed and looked up into his eyes. "Do you really want to try this? You and me? Dating?"

"There's nothing I've ever wanted more." He leaned in and gently kissed her seashell-pink lips. "Besides, you said you wanted to take more risks. I can't think of a bigger risk than to give your heart to someone."

She took in a deep breath. "Let's take it slow, okay?"

"Understood. I'll be like a snail."

At the indoor climbing wall in the nearby town of Mount Harmony, Drew felt as though he could scale the wall in record time—maybe even barefoot. When Janie agreed to give dating a try, he could barely contain the excitement. He wanted to shout it all over Whispering Slopes. Never in his wildest dreams did he believe he would ever feel this much joy and elation again. For the first time in two years, he actually looked forward to the future and it felt great.

"I know the excursions at your center will be out-doors, but it's smart of you to take our basic skills class so you can familiarize yourself with the sport. Since you both are beginners, we're going to climb that wall over there." Scott, the owner of the center, pointed across the room. "Those are what we call bouldering routes."

"I've heard that term, but could you explain it?" Drew requested after Janie gave him a questioning look.

"Sure. We call them bouldering routes because they are simply short rock climbing problems. You won't require any ropes or harnesses." He turned to Drew. "Since you said neither of you will actually be conduct-ing the climbs, this will be a great way for you to get a taste of what the climbers experience."

Janie looked at Drew. "This is going to be fun." She clapped her hands together and jumped up and down, just like Riley.

"That's what it's all about." Scott nodded. "Before we get started let's go fit you with some shoes and get chalk for your hands."

Standing at the bottom of the wall, Drew's feet felt like an orange inside of a juicer. "I think I've got the wrong size, Scott. These feel way too tight." He winced.

"The rock climbing shoes are made to feel snug. They have pointy toes so you can hang on to the edge of the rock a little easier," Scott explained. "Trust me, you'll get used to them."

"It looks so high." Janie glanced up toward the ceil-ing, holding her stomach.

Drew hoped Janie was ready for this. When they were in elementary school, she'd been afraid to walk across the high balance beam in gym class. "I'll let you go in front of me, in case you slip, I'll break your fall."

Janie playfully pushed Drew's shoulder. "Thanks for the vote of confidence. I'll probably beat you to the top."

"No one is going to fall. Just remember to push up from your legs. It might feel more natural to pull with your arms, but your thighs are stronger. You'll get more tired and probably won't make it to the top if you rely on arm strength, so use those legs. You want to plan each move, setting your feet before you move your hands. Keep your weight on your toes, instead of your hands," Scott instructed. "And most important of all, be deliberate and have fun."

Drew scratched his head. "And I thought all that we had to remember was not to look down."

Scott and Janie laughed as the threesome prepared for the climb.

"Oh here, I almost forgot." Scott passed them each a bag.

"What's this for?" Drew examined the satchel.

The instructor demonstrated by securing the belt around his waist and opening the bag. He tilted it to show the contents. "It's the chalk, to help keep your hands dry."

After what seemed like an eternity, Drew was three-quarters of the way to the top when his foot slipped and his heart skipped a beat. With his left hand, he wiped the sweat from his brow while holding on with his right hand. He'd forgotten Scott's instructions to use your legs, not your arms, so he was struggling a bit. He carefully dipped his wet hand inside the bag of chalk. Switching, he coated a light dusting on the other. Looking up, he saw Janie was on a roll. She seemed like a professional. "Well, now you're just being a show-off," he called out when she reached the top.

Janie looked down at Drew and Scott. "This is fun. I think I'd like to try the real thing."

Witnessing Janie stepping out of her comfort zone and enjoying herself made Drew happy. But the thought of her doing any real rock climbing in the mountains didn't sit well with him. He wouldn't want her to risk getting injured.

Finally, Scott and Drew reached the top. Scott turned to Janie. "Great job…you seem to be a natural, but remember, outdoor climbing is an entirely different world than climbing these walls indoors. You'll need to do a lot of training here before it would be safe for you to do the real thing."

Drew's shoulders relaxed as he listened to Scott point out the dangers of climbing. Drew didn't want to stop her from experiencing new things, but her safety was important to him.

"I might add this to my bucket list," Janie said as she began her descent.

On the car ride back to the farm, Janie could hardly sit still. "I can't believe I really did it, Drew. All of my life, I've been petrified of heights."

"I'm so proud of you. You seemed to breeze up the wall with little effort. You didn't look the least bit scared."

"The strange thing about it is, I really wasn't. I had faith in myself. It felt incredible." Janie's voice bubbled with joy. "Truthfully, I don't have a strong desire to do real rock climbing. I think I just wanted to prove to myself that I'm capable. Does that sound silly?"

Drew shook his head. "Not at all."

Once at the farm, Drew navigated his truck down the gravel road and pulled up in front of the barn. "I want to check to see if we need to order more oats for the horses."

Janie glanced at her watch. "Mrs. Buser should have Riley home any minute. I told her you were taking the group of children hiking this afternoon. She is so excited to go along."

Drew placed the vehicle into Park and unbuckled his seat belt. "How many kids are signed up?"

Janie exited the truck and stretched her arms over her head. "There're nine, including Riley. There're no other adults going. Are you sure you don't want me to come along to help?"

"No, by law we're good with the ratio, so I'll be fine. We'll only be out for an hour. Besides, I think it might be a good idea for you to follow up on the liability insurance and to make sure the CPR instructor has us on his schedule for next week. We've got to get all of the employees certified." Drew hoped he wasn't sounding like her boss. This was definitely a partnership.

Janie smiled. "Actually, I've got both of those items on my list of things to do today."

Drew leaned in and snuck a quick kiss. "This is why we're partners. We make a great team."

Two hours later, Janie tallied some receipts at her kitchen table while on hold with the insurance company. After twenty minutes, she pushed herself away from the paperwork and headed to the coffee maker. Pouring the leftovers from this morning into her cup, she popped it into the microwave as her mind drifted to the kiss she and Drew shared the night by the lake. Her heart warmed thinking about it. It had been the perfect kiss.

When the microwave beeped, Janie removed her beverage and headed back to her laptop. Her stomach knotted when an email popped up on her screen. Randy. Since she hadn't heard from him in a while, she'd hoped he'd been in contact with his lawyer to arrange visitation. There was nothing in the subject line, so against her better judgment, she opened the correspondence.

Dear Janie, Whether you like it or not, Riley is my daughter, too. I have the right to see her and I plan to exercise that right. Regards, Randy.

Janie read the email again and again. What did it mean? He planned to have his attorney try to seek custody? No. He'd said before he didn't want to settle this through lawyers. He thought they were a waste of money.

She massaged her fingers deep into her temples. Could he be here in Whispering Slopes? She closed her laptop. Running across the tile floor, she snatched her keys off the counter. She raced to the pantry and grabbed her purse, slinging it over her shoulder. After bolting toward the back door, she ran to her car. She had to find Riley before Randy. She didn't want to think he'd ever harm her, but his behavior could be unpredictable. Inside her car, she turned the key in the ignition and hit the accelerator hard, leaving the house in a cloud of dust.

As she navigated the curves, she prayed for Riley's safety. Should she have gone against her attorney's advice and responded to Randy's emails? Janie knew he got upset when he was ignored.

A few minutes into the drive, Janie realized she didn't know which trail Drew had taken the kids to this afternoon. He had mentioned his plan to let the children decide whether they wanted to hike the river trail or the one with several overlooks.

Think, Janie. She bit hard on her lower lip. Which trail would the kids prefer? Wait—her cell. She'd call Drew to find out where they were and also to give him a heads-up about Randy possibly being in the area. Flipping her turn signal, she exited off the road to make her call. She guided the car safely into Ben's Farmer's Market's parking lot. After unbuckling her seat belt, she lifted her purse off the passenger seat and fumbled for her phone. Not feeling the device inside of her bag, she dumped the contents onto the leather upholstery.

When the device was nowhere among her wallet, hand wipes, tissues and breath mints, Janie remembered she'd left it on the kitchen table next to her laptop. She crammed the items back inside her bag, flung it onto the seat and pulled back on to the road. Her thoughts went to Riley. If given the choice, which trail would she pick for the hike? *The water.* Riley loved to be near the river.

Janie released a steady breath and told herself her daughter would be okay. She had to be. As she headed in the direction of Sleepy Hollow Falls, a chill ran through her body as the sky opened up, sending fat raindrops before buckets came down. Turning on the wipers didn't improve the visibility. A wall of water confronted her. She reached for the defroster button and turned it on high, but the condensation on the windshield continued to spread. Leaning forward, Janie wiped her hand along the glass, but the smudges made it even more difficult to see. Common sense told her she should pull over, wait it out, but she had to make sure Riley was safe, so she compromised and released some pressure off of the accelerator. When the wheels skidded as the vehicle hugged a tight curve, Janie slowed a little more. If she had an accident, she would be of no help to Riley.

Thoughts of Randy confronting Drew camped out in her mind. Drew knew about the abuse. How would he react if he were to come face-to-face with Randy? Drew was protective, so the reaction wouldn't be a good one. What if they got into a fight in front of the children? She kicked herself for leaving her phone behind. She could only hope that once she got to the trail someone would be around and she could borrow their phone.

Thankfully, the farther she traveled along the road, the more the rain seemed to let up. Moments later, she had passed through the downpour and had reached dry pavement. There was no sign of the monsoon she'd just experienced.

Within minutes, Janie arrived at the parking lot located at the base of the trail. She looked around for the camp's van. Her shoulders relaxed for a brief moment when she spotted the vehicle at the far side of the parking lot. There was no sign of Randy's car or the vehicle Drew had described traveling down her driveway, but Randy could be driving a different rental. Had she overreacted in racing over here? But she had to be sure Riley was okay, so she stowed her purse in the back, out of sight, and locked the car. She sucked in a breath and headed toward the trail, hoping she'd find her daughter.

Fifteen minutes later, Janie slowed her pace. With no people around, she started to feel a little uneasy being out on an isolated trail alone. Not the smartest move. She whirled around at the sound of brush rustling behind her. Janie laughed at the two squirrels chasing each other before they scampered up a nearby oak tree. *Come on, Janie. You're scared of a couple little critters.* She shook off her fear and continued along the path. Sticks and leaves crunched underneath her tennis shoes. Drew wouldn't approve of her footwear.

A rumble of thunder in the distance sounded. Then seconds later, her blood turned cold when she heard Drew call out. She stopped in her tracks. Riley. Why was he calling for her daughter?

Janie sprinted up the path, losing her balance when her foot stubbed on a tree root. Her arms flailed as she gasped for a breath. She hit the ground hard, her wrist twisting under her weight, but she pushed through the pain. Back on her feet, she ran at top speed toward Drew's voice. Riley. Where was she?

Seconds later, she spotted Drew moving slowly down the path. The children trailed behind. Janie searched the group and her heart sank.

"Drew!" The ground beneath her feet spun. "Where is Riley?"

His shoulders slumped. He avoided eye contact.

Piercing pains shot through her chest. "Where is she?" Janie gripped Drew's forearms. She shook him, pleading for an answer.

Drew slowly raised his head before dropping to his knees. He dug his fingertips into the ground before he looked up to Janie with bloodshot eyes, his face painted blotchy red. "She's missing."

Chapter Eighteen

Beads of sweat trickled down Drew's neck as he rose to his feet. His tongue twisted. Riley was missing. How did he allow this to happen? He'd been responsible for her safety. Just like the accident. He'd failed to save his family and now he'd failed Janie.

"When did you last see Riley, Drew?" Janie's voice quivered.

"It's been thirty minutes, or so." His voice shook as he raked both hands through his hair, his mind reeling. "Jonathan fell. I was treating the cut and when I finished, she was gone. Julia said she'd chased after a rabbit. I tried to call you, but you didn't pick up." A tear seeped out of the corner of his eye. "I'm so sorry, Janie. This is my fault. Riley was my responsibility."

The rumbling of engines reached them.

Drew took a deep breath and rubbed his eyes. "Mark and a few guys from town have organized a search party. They're out on their four-wheelers. The sheriff's department is looking for her, too. They're going to put out an Amber Alert. They'll find her." Drew tried to reassure Janie. But he struggled to believe his own words.

"I think Randy might have taken her," Janie croaked.

Drew's chest tightened. "Has he contacted you again?"

She nodded. "He emailed me earlier. He said he had a right to see her." She paused to catch her breath. "And he planned to exercise the right. I should never have ignored him."

"Don't blame yourself, Janie. This is my fault. Riley was under my watch today." Drew prayed silently for Riley's safety before turning his attention back to Janie. "We need to get a picture of Randy over to the sheriff right away."

"But, I—I don't have any photographs of him." She tipped her head to the ground.

"What's wrong?"

Janie rolled her shoulders. "I burned all of the pictures when I left him." She hesitated. "Riley has one on her dresser, though."

"I'll call Mark and tell him we're heading over to your house to get the photo. I'll have Deputy Jacobs meet us at the farm. Laura Marie just got to the parking lot. She'll take the children." Drew slipped his phone from his pocket.

Five minutes later, inside his truck, Drew stole glances in Janie's direction. Her eyes closed and her lips moved. Drew didn't have to hear her words to know she was asking God to bring her daughter home. The guilt caused his stomach to churn. What if they couldn't find her?

Janie leaned her head against the back of the seat before turning to Drew. "After everything you've been through, I know what you're thinking, Drew, but please, don't blame yourself. Children wander off—it's what they do." Her voice was unsteady. "I know how Riley can react when she sees an animal."

Drew gripped the steering wheel as he rounded a curve, touched by Janie's words—her daughter was missing and she was trying to comfort him. "I love that little girl so much." He sucked in a breath. "If anything happens to Riley, I'll never forgive myself."

During the remainder of the trip the couple rode in silence. The clock was ticking. The more time that passed without Riley being found, the more Drew's guilt festered.

Gravel crunched underneath the tires of Drew's truck as they neared Janie's house.

"Look!" she shouted, pointing at the sheriff's car parked in the driveway. "They're already here."

Drew's tension eased. "I'm not surprised. The first responders in Whispering Slopes are top-notch." He ground his teeth back and forth. Of course, he couldn't say the same about himself. Drew thought he'd come to terms with the accident, but Riley going missing while he was responsible for her had once again sent him down the road of guilt and blame.

Drew jumped from the truck. He rounded the other side to open the door for Janie but she was quick. After springing from the vehicle, she raced up the walkway toward the two deputies who stood on the porch.

"Thank you for coming so quickly," Janie said.

An older deputy stepped forward and reached for Janie's forearm. "We're going to find Riley. Don't worry."

Drew looked at the older gentleman. "Janie, this is Deputy Williamson."

"Please, call me Charlie." He turned to his partner. "This is Deputy Harper, but you can call him Joel. We're all family in this town."

Drew watched as the tension seemed to ease from Janie's face. "Let's head inside and get these fellas that photograph."

Gathered around the kitchen table, Janie explained to the deputies the issues surrounding her divorce and the emails she'd been receiving from Randy. She also mentioned possibly seeing him at the fair and Drew spotting the strange vehicle on her driveway before it made an abrupt U-turn. She'd powered on her laptop to show them the emails from Randy.

"At the start of my career, I worked in New York City. We handled these kinds of cases all of the time," the older deputy said after studying the messages. "Of course, here in Whispering Slopes, it's rare, but I'd say Riley is with your ex-husband. This is a good thing given the fact that he's never harmed her in the past. The tone of his emails sounds to me like a man who has a lot of regrets and he wants to right the situation, but he's not quite sure how. He mentioned he's been seeing a therapist for the last ten months, so that's a good sign."

Drew appreciated Charlie's take on the situation. He tried to ease Janie's worries, but it didn't take away from the facts. Riley was missing because of him. Drew's shoulders were laden with burden. He knew the truth. He'd fulfilled Mrs. Applegate's last wishes. Janie and Riley had a home and a potentially thriving business. Their future was bright. Drew couldn't risk ruining that for the two people who mattered most in the world to him. He had to protect Janie and her daughter. With a heavy heart, he knew what he had to do. Terminating his partnership with Janie and closing the door on the dream of owning an outdoor sports center was the only way to make this wrong right again.

Hunkered down in the kitchen, Janie poured a fresh cup of coffee for the deputies and passed each a steaming beverage. Since they'd scanned the photo of Randy on her printer and emailed it to their headquarters, the men had been on their phones nonstop.

Charlie took a sip. "The photo has been distributed all over the valley." He reached for Janie's hand. "Relax. It's only a matter of time."

Janie prayed this was true. She turned toward the front window where Drew had planted himself for the past thirty minutes. Her heart ached for him. Drew felt responsible for Riley. But how could she help him?

Slowly, Janie approached Drew and joined him. "Can I get you some coffee?"

He shook his head and kept a close eye on the outside, like a lighthouse keeper with a strong nor'easter in the forecast.

"Talk to me, Drew. What's going through your mind?" Janie pleaded.

He turned and reached for both of her hands. "I'm going to dissolve our partnership for the center. I can give you the money to go forward on your own, or we can let it go. I should have never gotten you involved in this."

Janie knew he was distraught over Riley's disappearance, but this? She never imagined he'd give up on their plan. "But it's your dream. We were going to make it come true together, as a team." Her eyes moistened.

"I'm better off on my own. I'm no good for you."

Janie's heart sank right along with the future she'd seen so clearly. The future she'd prayed for.

Charlie entered the room and stepped toward the couple. "Excuse me, but we just got a call on a reported sighting. A man fitting Randy's description, along with a child, left a restaurant in Lexington about an hour ago. This is good news, Janie." Charlie placed his hand on her arm. "He's staying in the area. I have a feeling he plans to bring her home."

Janie pushed Drew's decision out of her mind. She had to keep her thoughts on what was most important... Riley. After grabbing a cup of coffee, she headed down the hall to her bedroom to pray.

Over the next half an hour, Janie sat in her reading chair and asked God to return her daughter home safe. She prayed Drew would rely on His strength to sustain him and that He would provide the wisdom to realize that their lives were not their own. Everything happening around them, both the good and the bad, was working together for a greater good. She knew this to be true. Finally, she prayed for Randy.

The wall clock clicked, counting the hours Riley had been missing. Janie pulled the angora blanket from the back of the chair, and wrapped it tight around her shoulders. The house was still with the exception of occasional murmurs by the deputies. Seconds later, Janie heard the front door open.

"Mommy! Mommy! I'm home!"

Janie sprang from the seat, her heart rate tripling in speed. She took off down the hall, never moving so fast in her life. Her prayers had been answered. Rounding the corner, she broke into tears at the sight of her sweet little girl's face.

With her arms wide-open, Riley ran to Janie. "Mommy! I had the best time in the world with Daddy!"

Janie held on to her daughter with everything she had. She was safe and that was all that mattered. With her face buried into Riley's pixie-cut hair, she glanced up to catch the back side of Drew before he slipped out the front door. Numb, she heard the car engine start outside then fade into the distance, taking her heart along with it. Had she lost him forever?

Following an hour of discussion with the deputies and Randy, Janie decided not to press charges against her ex-husband.

"I handled everything wrong today, Janie. I should have done this properly, through our attorneys. I've been in counseling and I know I have a lot more work to do, but I realize the way I treated you during our marriage was totally unacceptable. I'm ashamed of myself. I know God has forgiven me, but it's taking me a little longer to forgive myself. And today, I should have never taken Riley without your permission, but I had to see her. I couldn't wait for the attorneys to draw up an agreement. Being with her today has made everything clear. I want to be a part of her life and I'm willing to do whatever it takes to make that happen." A stray tear slipped down Randy's cheek.

Throughout their marriage, Janie had never seen her husband cry. Randy had grown up in an abusive household. She'd always assumed he'd used up all of his tears. Sitting across from him, watching him confess his wrongs, she felt sorry for him.

Riley slipped into the kitchen where the adults were gathered around the table. Tiptoeing toward her mother, she tugged on her arm. "Don't be mad at Daddy. He just wanted to spend some time with me. He's sorry he didn't ask for permission," Riley pleaded, her eyes red with tears. "Mrs. Buser told me that God says we should love everyone, even those who've done wrong things. He says to pray for people who mistreat us. Can't we just pray for Daddy and not be angry?"

In awe of the child's words, the grown-ups sat speechless.

Janie straightened her shoulders. She'd never been prouder of her daughter. Scooping her up into her arms, she smothered Riley with kisses. "You're right, sweetie."

Two hours and many tears later, Janie and Randy had discussed their past and what would happen moving forward. Janie insisted if Randy wanted to spend time with Riley, he must first undergo a psychological evaluation and then the court could appoint a supervisor for visitation. He agreed and was willing to do whatever was necessary to have a relationship with Riley. They planned to contact their attorneys to get the process started.

Janie watched out the window as Riley wiped away the tears before giving her father a hug goodbye. Riley's feet stayed planted as he drove up the driveway and the deputies got into their vehicles. Janie prayed that one day Riley would understand her mother had to do what was best for her daughter. There were consequences to Randy's actions. Janie felt at peace to allow the court to make the decision regarding visitation.

Her thoughts drifted to Drew and the pain she'd seen in his eyes when he told her Riley was missing. She knew what she had to do.

For the next hour, Janie sent a brief email to her divorce attorney to explain what had transpired. She cleared away the coffee cups and wiped down the kitchen countertops. Finally, she rounded up Riley. As they headed outside to her vehicle, Janie explained where they were going.

Behind the wheel of the car, Janie glanced at her rearview mirror, watching Randy and the deputies talking in the driveway. As she moved away from her past, she had to trust that she and Riley were moving toward a bright future.

"Is Mr. Drew mad at me, Mommy?" Riley peered out the backseat window.

Janie eyed her daughter in the mirror. "No, sweetie, he was worried about you—that's all." She had to believe this. Janie had to trust that everything would be okay between her and Drew. It had to be. She loved him and she wanted nothing more than to spend the rest of her life with him. And in that moment, she knew what she had to do. It was time for her to step out of her comfort zone and take control of her life.

When they arrived at Drew's cabin, Janie's emotions were like a hummingbird flitting from flower to flower in search of the sweetest nectar. Though excited to share her feelings with him, she was concerned he wanted to pull away from her and their business venture. Their outdoor adventure company she could live without, but a life without Drew would be impossible.

Janie exhaled a lungful of air and knocked on the front door. *You can do this.*

Footsteps sounded on the other side of the cedar door before it slowly opened. "Janie?" Drew's brow knitted together.

In that second, it dawned on her, she'd never been to his home. Of course he'd be surprised to see her.

"Can we come in, Drew?" Her heart pounded an erratic rhythm. Dressed in black sweat shorts that brushed his knees and a Washington Nationals baseball jersey that accentuated his muscular arms, he looked gorgeous.

"Sure, come on in." He opened the door a little wider before looking down at Riley. "Hey, munchkin."

Janie observed Riley's abnormal behavior. Usually in Drew's presence she'd get excited, but now, she seemed timid as she cowered behind her mother.

Drew turned to Janie. "What's wrong?"

"Riley thinks you're upset with her since she didn't tell you she was going to have lunch with her father," Janie explained.

Drew bent down in front of the little girl, taking her hands into his own. "I was concerned about your safety, munchkin. No way in the world would I be mad at you…you're my BFF."

Riley giggled, throwing her arms around him. "You're my best friend forever too, Mr. Drew!"

"I'm just relieved you're okay." Drew poked Riley's tummy before standing. "I'm sorry I left without saying goodbye. I thought the three of you needed some time alone."

"We had a good talk. Riley knows to never leave with anyone when she's under someone else's supervision. Randy and I agreed to a visitation schedule, so he won't be sneaking around," Janie explained.

Drew nodded and lowered his gaze, but his silence lingered.

Janie realized he still harbored guilt from Riley's disappearance. How could she make him understand it wasn't his fault? Then she remembered a time she'd felt the same way. "You know, when we lived in Maryland,

Riley and I had gone to the mall to do a little back-to-school shopping. The place was packed. I'd run into an old friend and while we were chatting at the cosmetic counter Riley had spotted her girlfriend out in the mall and wandered away. Just like you, I was frantic. How could a mother allow her child to just disappear? What kind of mother was I? Thankfully, I found her safe and I learned that sometimes, no matter how hard we try to protect our children, we're only human and we're going to make mistakes." She reached out, gently touching his arm.

Drew turned his focus back to Riley and smiled. "You really scared me, squirt."

"I'm sorry, Mr. Drew." She stood in front of him and with her index finger, motioned for him.

Drew knelt in front of the child.

Riley placed her tiny hands on Drew's cheeks. "My Mommy told me you had a little girl who was the same age as me."

Drew's gaze remained on the child. He never blinked. "That's true. Her name was Heidi."

Riley looked up toward the ceiling as a tear slipped from the corner of her eye. "I'm sorry she's not here anymore."

"I'm sorry, too." Drew's voice trailed off into nothingness.

Janie considered her daughter as Riley studied Drew's face.

"I think me and Heidi would have been really good friends. Don't you?"

Drew immediately scooped Riley into his arms, burying his face into her shoulders. Seconds later, he pulled back and wiped his eyes with his forearm. "I think you would have been lifelong friends."

Janie pressed her palms against her chest. She wanted to remember this moment forever. Watching Drew and her daughter made her heart full. If she didn't confess her feelings now, she'd lose her nerve. "Riley came here to apologize, but I'm here for completely selfish reasons, Drew."

Two lines creased in his forehead as he stood. "What do you mean?"

She took his hands, pulling him closer. "You can't give up your dream of owning an outdoor adventure center, just like I can't give up on my happily-ever-after. I love you, Drew Brenner. I want to share every adventure life has to offer with you."

A slow grin parted Drew's lips. "What are you saying, Janie?"

Ignoring the flip-flops deep in her belly, she pulled in a steadying breath. No longer the timid and frightened woman, she felt strong in Drew's presence. He gave her strength. "I'm not saying—I'm asking. Will you marry me, Drew?"

Squeals and clapping echoed inside the cabin. "Yeah! That was awesome, Mommy!"

Drew's eyes widened and fixed on Janie. "Hey, I thought I was the one who was supposed to ask?" He winked before he swept Janie into his arms and gently pressed his lips to hers. "I love you, too. There's nothing in life I want more than to share my life with you and Riley."

Epilogue

Drew squinted in the bright sunlight as he watched Janie steady her core before gripping the final rock of their climb. *Janie*. His wife. After she'd surprised him with a wedding proposal eleven months earlier, Drew's world had been a whirlwind of wedding plans and arranging for the grand opening of Rocky River Camp and Outdoor Adventures.

Their ceremony was held outside on a picturesque day. The couple had exchanged vows in front of family and friends on the opening day of their new partnership. It seemed the perfect venue as the two set off on the most exciting adventure of all. The scars on her arms no longer kept a secret, Janie had worn a striking sleeveless wedding dress with a stunning beaded, deep-V neckline.

Janie hoisted herself up with a sense of self-confidence Drew had seen blossom over the past year. "I did it!" She planted both feet on the ground in front of her husband and placed her hands on her narrow hips.

"I never had any doubts, Mrs. Brenner." Drew scooped his bride into his arms and twirled, both laughing. "I have a feeling being married to you will be one big adventure after another."

With her feet back on the ground, Janie's eyes grew serious. "Do you think you're ready for that, Drew?"

He nodded. "I know when you and Riley first came to Whispering Slopes you and I were both kind of a mess. Of course, I was a bigger mess." He chuckled. "But seriously, I had always believed everything in life could be planned. Then the accident changed it all. Living life without a road map seemed too risky. I needed to know what tomorrow would bring." Drew reached for his wife's hands. "You made me realize life doesn't always turn out the way we planned, but that's okay because it does go on. You brought me back to life, Mrs. Brenner." He lightly pressed his lips to hers. "So to answer your question, yes, I've never been more ready."

A smile parted her lips. "Well, you better hold on to those climbing boots, Drew. I'm about to take you on the most exciting adventure of all." She tilted her head. Janie pulled his hand and gently placed it across her stomach. "I went to the doctor today. We're going to have a baby, Drew."

"What? How—"

Janie laughed.

"I'm sorry. I mean...I don't know what I mean. A baby! We're going to have a baby?" Drew paused for a second, allowing the news to take hold and his heart rate to slow. He gently brushed Janie's hair away from her face and stared into his wife's eyes, now peppered with tears. "Well, it looks like with God's help, our dear friend Mrs. Applegate's plan went exactly how she had hoped."

* * * * *

If you enjoyed this story, don't miss Jill Weatherholt's next emotional romance, available next year from Love Inspired!

Find more great reads at www.LoveInspired.com

Dear Reader,

Welcome back to Whispering Slopes! I enjoyed writing this story about Drew and Janie—two people who learned that life doesn't always turn out the way we planned.

I always liked the saying, *"Man plans, God laughs,"* because we can't always plan everything. Life can be messy and full of disappointment. People aren't perfect, but that's okay. And the past doesn't have to determine our destiny. Instead, we can choose to focus on God's promises and allow Him to direct our steps rather than trying to control everything.

So today, let go and let God! He'll surprise you with new opportunities and dreams you could never even imagine, just like He did for Drew and Janie.

I love to hear from readers. Please visit my website and sign up for my newsletter at jillweatherholt.com. Or email me at authorjillweatherholt@gmail.com. I'd love to chat with you.

Jill Weatherholt

WE HOPE YOU ENJOYED
THIS BOOK FROM

LOVE INSPIRED
INSPIRATIONAL ROMANCE

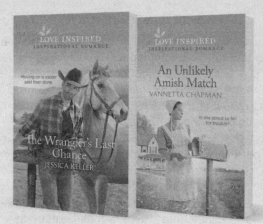

Uplifting stories of faith, forgiveness and hope.

Fall in love with stories where faith helps guide you through life's challenges, and discover the promise of a new beginning.

6 NEW BOOKS AVAILABLE EVERY MONTH!

THE AMISH CHRISTMAS SECRET
Indiana Amish Brides • by Vannetta Chapman
Becca Schwartz is positive something's off with her next-door neighbor. Why would Daniel Glick move to the only farm worse than her family's if he can afford an exquisite new horse? Her focus must stay on her family's desperate financial straits. But as she falls for Daniel, his secret could change her life forever...

THE AMISH WIDOW'S CHRISTMAS HOPE
Amish of Serenity Ridge • by Carrie Lighte
When single mother Fern Glick inherits her uncle's home at Christmastime, she has no intention of living in the same town as widower Walker Huyard—her ex-fiancé who left her to marry her cousin. But can he convince her to stay without breaking his promise to never reveal certain details of the past?

THE COWBOY'S CHRISTMAS BLESSINGS
Wyoming Sweethearts • by Jill Kemerer
Offering a cabin to a friend in need and her triplet babies for the holidays is an easy decision for rancher Judd Wilson. But when Nicole Taylor insists on helping him build a gingerbread house for his aunt to return the favor, can he avoid losing his heart to the single mother?

FINDING HER CHRISTMAS FAMILY
Golden Grove • by Ruth Logan Herne
Only one thing stands between Sarah and her late sister's daughters this Christmas: Renzo Calloway, their deputy sheriff guardian. Sarah never even knew her sister existed until recently, and Renzo is the only family her nieces know. Together, can they build a future that includes the girls...and each other?

ALASKAN CHRISTMAS REDEMPTION
Home to Owl Creek • by Belle Calhoune
Struggling to keep her diner afloat through the holidays, Piper Miller turns to her best friend, Braden North, for help. But as they work together to find ways to revitalize her business, Braden must keep the truth about a tragedy from their past hidden...or risk losing Piper for good.

UNEXPECTED CHRISTMAS JOY
by Gabrielle Meyer
Actress Kate LeClair doesn't know the first thing about babies, yet she's just become the guardian of eighteen-month-old triplets. Asking experienced single father Pastor Jacob Dawson for help with the little boys might just give Kate the greatest Christmas gift of all—family.

Get 4 FREE REWARDS!

We'll send you 2 FREE Books plus 2 FREE Mystery Gifts.

Love Inspired books feature uplifting stories where faith helps guide you through life's challenges and discover the promise of a new beginning.

FREE
Value Over
$20

YES! Please send me 2 FREE Love Inspired Romance novels and my 2 FREE mystery gifts (gifts are worth about $10 retail). After receiving them, if I don't wish to receive any more books, I can return the shipping statement marked "cancel." If I don't cancel, I will receive 6 brand-new novels every month and be billed just $5.24 each for the regular-print edition or $5.99 each for the larger-print edition in the U.S., or $5.74 each for the regular-print edition or $6.24 each for the larger-print edition in Canada. That's a savings of at least 13% off the cover price. It's quite a bargain! Shipping and handling is just 50¢ per book in the U.S. and $1.25 per book in Canada.* I understand that accepting the 2 free books and gifts places me under no obligation to buy anything. I can always return a shipment and cancel at any time. The free books and gifts are mine to keep no matter what I decide.

Choose one: ☐ **Love Inspired Romance**
Regular-Print
(105/305 IDN GNWC)

☐ **Love Inspired Romance**
Larger-Print
(122/322 IDN GNWC)

Name (please print)

Address   Apt. #

City   State/Province   Zip/Postal Code

Email: Please check this box ☐ if you would like to receive newsletters and promotional emails from Harlequin Enterprises ULC and its affiliates. You can unsubscribe anytime.

> **Mail to the Reader Service:**
> **IN U.S.A.:** P.O. Box 1341, Buffalo, NY 14240-8531
> **IN CANADA:** P.O. Box 603, Fort Erie, Ontario L2A 5X3

Want to try 2 free books from another series! Call 1-800-873-8635 or visit www.ReaderService.com.

---

*Terms and prices subject to change without notice. Prices do not include sales taxes, which will be charged (if applicable) based on your state or country of residence. Canadian residents will be charged applicable taxes. Offer not valid in Quebec. This offer is limited to one order per household. Books received may not be as shown. Not valid for current subscribers to Love Inspired Romance books. All orders subject to approval. Credit or debit balances in a customer's account(s) may be offset by any other outstanding balance owed by or to the customer. Please allow 4 to 6 weeks for delivery. Offer available while quantities last.

Your Privacy—Your information is being collected by Harlequin Enterprises ULC, operating as Reader Service. For a complete summary of the information we collect, how we use this information and to whom it is disclosed, please visit our privacy notice located at corporate.harlequin.com/privacy-notice. From time to time we may also exchange your personal information with reputable third parties. If you wish to opt out of this sharing of your personal information, please visit readerservice.com/consumerschoice or call 1-800-873-8635. **Notice to California Residents**—Under California law, you have specific rights to control and access your data. For more information on these rights and how to exercise them, visit corporate.harlequin.com/california-privacy.

LI20R2